SECRET WORDS

LORRAINE ROPOSH BERAN

Lorraine Roposh Beran

email: lorrainelberan@gmail.com
twitter: @beranlorraine
blog: rainydaypublications.wordpress.com

Copyright ©2015 by Lorraine Roposh Beran

All rights reserved. No part of this book may be used or reproduced in any manner whatsoever without written permission of the author.

Printed in the United States of America.

ISBN: 978-1-63385-078-1
Library of Congress Control Number: 2015908969

Published by

Word Association Publishers
205 Fifth Avenue
Tarentum, Pennsylvania 15084

www.wordassociation.com
1.800.827.7903

The cornerstone of my life is faith and family.
Both give meaning to my life and inspire my writing.

My family is an integral part of this book; the personalities of my husband, my three children, my daughter-in-law, and my two grandsons are woven into every character. How could they not be? It would be impossible for me to separate my love for them from my love for the characters I created.

I am grateful for my family's unwavering confidence in my abilities, and I thank them for being alongside me during my journey.

Chapter 1

I CUPPED MY HANDS UNDER THE TAP of the bathroom sink, and tepid water cascaded through my fingertips. I bent down and slurped the water and aimlessly splashed some around my mouth. The lukewarm water, mixed with some of the toothpaste that still coated my teeth, rolled down my throat. When I raised my head, I closed my eyes to avoid my reflection in the mirror. I kept them shut and just listened.

My heart beat in my ears, and it was a wonderful distraction. I thought of all the sounds of life that fill every moment of the day. The buzz of traffic, the tingle of wind chimes, the swoosh of a plastic grocery bag, the cacophony of voices. There are so many noises around us that we become numb to the drone of machines and electronic gadgets; even the soothing sounds of nature become muddled in the chatter and clatter of everyday life.

Silence, on the other hand, is strangely noticeable. Even a hint of quiet makes people uncomfortable and anxious. We try to fill any second of noiselessness with background music or television noise.

So I wondered: Is anyone even aware that I have said so little in the past week? Are they too busy, or don't they care enough to even notice?

I admit that I had grunted and nodded occasionally. I had also emailed a few brief messages to concerned friends. But, not many real words have been uttered from my mouth for almost five days.

I suppose my parents have not questioned my quiet because they want to give me room to grieve. They haven't made any demands on me or tried to press me into a conversation. My brother and my friends have given me that same respect. They are all frightened. They don't know what to say to me and are probably afraid of what I might say to them.

All of them, friends and family, have given me space since the funeral. Out of fear, out of respect. But, honestly, I wonder if they really noticed my lack of communication. The only person who would have cared about my silence is gone. The sound of her voice taken away from me.

How beautiful the silence
The sound of nothing fills my ears.
Like a lovely vase
waiting to be filled with summer flowers,
I await the sound of your voice.

Of course, my family isn't exactly a bunch of great communicators. They have been supportive and caring, and I am grateful for that. But, just like many families, we often find ourselves too busy to have real conversations.

My dad, Wayne L. Harrison, is a thinker and a reader. A book, a newspaper, a magazine always beside him. A laptop open within reach. He's tall and slim, and people often remark that his graying brown hair makes him look distinguished. He's not much of a conversationalist, and many of his words are actually directed at the TV or his computer. He likes to make comments about the latest news events and the general state of the world today: "What's the matter with people today?" "Doesn't anybody read history books? That country will always be in a state of turmoil." Or, he yells at players, managers, referees—anyone connected with the particular game he is watching on TV. "Change the pitcher!" "Great play, let's do it again."

My mom is a talker, but not always a great listener. She bounces from subject to subject. Her athletic build and short auburn hair suit her firecracker, multitasking personality. Her favorite topics usually include religion, neighborhood events, and nostalgic stories about my and my brother's childhood. She's full of questions for me: "Leo, what would you like for dinner?" "Did you take out the garbage yet?" "What happened at school today?" Honestly though, she nags Brandon and my dad even more. She doesn't even let herself off the hook. When she's all alone in the kitchen or working at her desk, she even reprimands herself. "Really, Joyce, you did that stupid thing again?" "Concentrate, Joyce, or you'll never get finished!"

My older brother, Brandon, is a charmer. But he saves his charm for his friends, teachers, and coaches. When he talks at home, it's usually in a fast-paced, I'm-in-a-hurry type of voice. It's like hearing the snippets about upcoming news reports on television. "Game tonight. Back at nine." "See ya later. Going swimming with the guys."

Brandon is sixteen, barely two years older than I am, and he is considered a star athlete. He inherited our mom's athletic frame. His strong physique and short hair give him a military look, and he keeps that type of discipline in his sports life. He plays almost every sport, but he excels in ice hockey and baseball. He is rarely serious, and people are attracted to his energetic, fun-loving personality. Though academics are not his priority, he maintains an above-average GPA at North Central High. My parents and I spend much of our time supporting him at his games, and his schedule is always updated and posted on the fridge. Most of our family discussions center around Brandon and his activities.

As for my athletic career, I play golf, swim, and run intramural track. Those sports are more aligned with the tall, slim build that makes me an acorn from my father's tree. They are also more in tune with my personality. I shy away from the more competitive, high-profile sports. That means I have to answer some questions from friends and family: "When are you signing up for the hockey team?" "Hey, Leo, can you skate as good as your brother?" and, "Why aren't you out there on the ice?"

My answer is usually something like, "Brandon is the athlete in the family, and I want to focus more on my schoolwork." Most people shut up after that and figure I'm just a nerd who doesn't care about sports. But, there is a great deal of truth to my answer. Brandon and I are two very different species. And, here's some more truth . . . it doesn't bother me. I really like my brother. He's older, and he looks after me in his own brotherly way. We don't share feelings or anything, but I know that in most situations, he has my back.

So, my days of unspoken words passed without much awareness from anyone. My only true friend died, and, since her funeral, there doesn't seem to be anything real important for me to say. If someone asks me something, a shoulder shrug, an eye roll, or a grunt seem to work. I can bury my head in a book or wear earbuds and pretend to listen to music to stop any attempt at conversation. But, tomorrow the rather mute Leo will probably utter some words or even complete sentences. Summer vacation is over, and orientation for my new school begins.

I will be joining my brother in the grand halls of North Central Diocese High School all the way across town. It is almost ten miles from the public school that sits within a few miles of our house. It is a long standing Harrison tradition that all males become North Central Dragons. I need to make the adjustment from a regular public grade school to an all-male parochial school environment. My commute across town will be in some heavy traffic, so it will take at least thirty minutes. Starting tomorrow I'll set the alarm for six every day so that I can be at the bus stop by six thirty.

Orientation tomorrow is just for the incoming freshman class. My brother will be able to sleep in for another two days and then report with the junior class. The great thing is that no one from my public middle school is attending North Central, and the only people who will know me are Brandon and some of his friends. Why is anonymity such a great thing? At least no one in my new class will know that I have any connection to Jessie Delaney, the girl who was hit by a car and died.

Jessie's school friends will be in the same building as we all were last year. It is a seventh, eighth, and ninth grade public middle school. I heard that they are planning a short memorial service for Jessie on the opening day of school. The news stations have already mentioned the plans for the memorial.

Her funeral was difficult enough for me. I'm glad I won't have to bear another public reminder of her death.

Thoughts about Jessie and about life in general interrupted my focus often nowadays. I barely noticed that water was still dripping from the tap in the bathroom sink. After shutting it off, I used the back of my hand and part of my tee shirt to wipe the water from my face. I still averted my eyes from the mirror, too afraid to see any reminder of my own sadness.

I walked to my bedroom and sat on the edge of my bed. It was late enough in the evening for me to get to bed, especially since I had to get up by six the next morning. Out of habit, I grabbed my iPod and inserted the ear buds. My iPod was not even on, but I was still avoiding conversations with anyone in my family. My mom was always checking on me, and right now I just wanted to think—think about Jessie.

Chapter 2

EVEN AFTER ALL THE RECENT SADNESS, my memories of Jessie still make me smile. My mind often drifts back to the day and the moment that I knew Jessie would be my friend.

She was one of the prettiest girls in our class. She had long brown hair that framed her face and highlighted her green eyes. She was always smiling—a playful, honest smile that sucked you into her happiness. Jessie had this way of making everyone comfortable around her, as if you knew her all your life. Even though I had seen her around our school, I did not get to know her until we were in the seventh grade.

I didn't belong to many school clubs, but I did sign up to help out at the concession stand for our school basketball games. Lucky for me, Jessie signed up that year too. We were both assigned to work the first basketball game of the season. Our job was to set up the stand, replenish any items that were running low, and then clean up once the game was over. They usually only assigned the ninth graders and parents to sell stuff and handle money. The profits helped to support the team.

Jessie and I carried boxes into the gymnasium area where the soda and snacks were sold. It was a small room with an open section and counter for customers to make their purchases. Since this was the first game, we had a lot of prep work to do. Two of our teachers, Mr. Snead and Mr. Kowolski, were trying to change a fluorescent light bulb in the center of the ceiling. They were fumbling with the light panel and the ladder and were pretty much making all teachers look inept and stupid. I had just placed my box of paper plates on the counter when Jessie entered and stood by the doorway.

She stood there for a while watching the two stooges. In a voice just loud enough for everyone in the room to hear, she said, "Hey, Leo, how many teachers does it take to change a light bulb?"

I picked up her cue and played along.

"I don't know," I said in the same tone. "How many teachers does it take to change a light bulb?"

"More than two," she said as she shook her head in dramatic disgust. "More than two."

We guffawed and made exaggerated snorting sounds, enjoying the moment. Mr. Snead and Mr. Kowolski laughed too. Jessie had sucked us into her happy state, and it felt so good that I knew I wanted to stay there forever. I could feel my heart rate quicken and my armpits start to sweat. I felt a special bond with her that very second. I tried to look cool and calm, but her smile and her laugh were like adrenaline. I had to go to the boy's room and calm myself down with some deep breathing before I could return to the concession stand.

We finished our stocking task and got things in their proper positions for sale. Jessie checked off the inventory that we used, gave me a quick wave, and sat with some of her girlfriends to watch the game. I sat behind our team's bench with some of my friends.

When the game was over and the players and fans left, we grabbed brooms and dust pans and swept up the litter in the gym. We talked a little about our teachers and classes. She told me that her mom was coming to pick her up in ten minutes.

"Leo, you only live around the corner from me. You want a ride with us?"

That was the beginning of our friendship. Occasionally her mom or mine would drive us to school in the morning. After school, we took the bus home, and we always sat together. I started getting off at her stop, walking her part of the way to her door, and then continuing around the corner to my house. We didn't bother too much with each other during actual school time. She had girl friends around her, and I stuck with the guys.

Our real relationship began when we started to send emails to one another in the evenings. The topics were all over the board, but mostly they stayed light-hearted and silly.

However, that year around the end of November, Jessie sent me an email that had a different tone. She asked me if I enjoyed poetry, and if I would care to read a poem she had recently written. My mind took a dangerous turn as I anticipated a mushy love poem all about me, but the poem was definitely not a profession of her amorous feelings. The email had the title "Transitions."

Slithering little caterpillar,
not so pleasant to the eye,
Soon,
In a cocoon,
Your grounded life will die.
Your rainbow wings will open
To a life where you will fly.

I stared at the computer and read the poem over and over again. I pictured the caterpillar, and then the butterfly with Jessie's face. Her long brown hair swirled in the wind and her face smiled as she soared from flower to flower.

My head spun with worries about how to respond to her poetry. I knew that she had shared something special with me, something from her heart. An email that said, "Beautiful! Thanks for sharing," would not cut it.

My return email was titled "Beginnings."

Lovely rainbowed butterfly
Do not fear the sky.
It is a new beginning
So spread your wings and fly.

Jessie, your beautiful poem inspired me!

My hand hovered over the keys and shakily pressed "send." Immediately I regretted the choice. I hadn't refined or carefully proofread my work. What was I thinking? She would probably think I was trying to one-up her or ridicule her. My stomach was churning, and I wondered if I should send another email. "Hey, just joking with ya" or "What did you have for dinner?" or "You know, I'm just a stupid assed kid with no brain!" Minutes passed before I heard the bleep indicating an email had arrived. It was labeled "You."

You are my best friend. I knew I could share with you. Goodnight, Leo.

Sleep did not come quickly that night. I remember staring out of my window and wishing I could hold Jessie's hand and walk silently along a beach somewhere.

We wouldn't need to speak because we were one soul and one heart.

That was the beginning of seventh grade. As the year progressed we became much closer. Our emails became longer and longer. Strangely we shared more in our writing than in our spoken words. Our conversations were usually silly and playful; the emails serious and profound. We had no shyness about revealing our feelings and our thoughts.

We wrote poems to one another—enough poetry to publish a book. Any topic and every topic became a catalyst for a poem. Jessie excelled at her use of imagery and metaphor, and each poem put my little rhymes to shame. I spent many hours trying to read between the lines. I wanted to understand everything about her, but the only thing I really understood was that I loved her.

Chapter 3

THE ALARM STARTLED ME AWAKE with Aretha Franklin singing "Respect." What an omen for freshman orientation! My body was not accustomed to rising before ten, so I was a little slow in my morning routine. As I dressed, my mom kept yelling at me to hurry so I would make the bus. She wouldn't be able to drive me to North Central—the commute was too far, and it would make her late for work.

My mom had started back to her school last week. She is a middle school teacher in a neighboring school district, and she had been busy preparing for her classes to start in a few days. It was still a week before Labor Day, so most schools had not yet opened their doors to students.

I grabbed a breakfast bar from the pantry as my mom urged me to carry a backpack for the day.

"It's important to be prepared, Leo. You're in high school, and teachers might give you textbook assignments on your first day."

I'm sure her real plan was to pack me a snack and put some cutesy little note of encouragement inside the backpack. But I held my ground and carried only a mechanical pencil in my back pocket.

"You don't have to treat me like a child!" I said in disgust and anger. I've got what we were told to bring, Mom. The information letter said that there were no real classes the first day. Just a walk-through of our schedule and some speeches and stuff."

She rolled her eyes in defeat, looking surprised at my anger. "I'm just worried for you. I can't believe my baby is starting high school."

That conversation, if you could call it that, was the first one I had with her since the funeral. Before I was forced into more of an argument or a half-hearted apology, my mother glanced up at the kitchen clock.

"Leo, you need to hurry. You are the only person at that bus stop, and you don't want to piss off the bus driver on the first day!"

Wow! My mom rarely said "pissed," so I knew she was more worried about my first day of high school than I realized. I flew out the door and ran down the street.

Not only was I the only person at my stop, I was the only person riding the bus. This day was only for orientation, so it turned out that I was the only North Central freshman on this route. Bus driver Joe and I were buddies by the time the bus arrived at school. During the half-hour ride, Joe spent most of the time talking about his "crazy wife" and the many "wild-assed lunatic kids" he had to transport on his route.

Joe warned me, "You'll see soon enough, when school starts for those bums next week. Enjoy your peace and quiet while you can, kid."

He probably looked at my preppy khaki pants and red polo shirt and figured I wasn't going to be much of a problem. School uniforms always give the illusion of a disciplined, respectful young adult. Of course Joe would have no trouble from me, but I couldn't vouch for other kids in uniforms.

Halfway through another story about a brutal fight on one of his bus routes, Joe pulled the bus up to the hallowed doors of North Central Diocese High School. A long, wide banner bearing a flaming dragon and the words "Faith, Honor, and Diligence" draped above the huge double doors. A smaller sign was posted on the wall: "Freshmen, enter through side door."

The side door led directly to the auditorium, and, after my eyes adjusted to the dim light, I could make out the almost one hundred students who would now be the new freshmen class. As expected, nobody looked facially familiar. But, with everyone in brand new uniforms, we did look like drones from some cheap sci-fi movie.

I was scanning the room looking for an empty seat when a balding man in shorts grabbed my arm and guided me toward the center aisle. He turned out to be the phys ed teacher, and he handed me a packet of papers in a manila envelope.

"Sit down, son, this shindig is about to begin. You can fill out your name tag when the lights come back on."

I squeezed beside some guys who looked as lost as I felt. I barely sat down when someone asked for silence. Immediately the room went quiet. The discipline was stiff at North Central, and rarely did any direction have to be given twice.

We were formally greeted by the vice-principal, Miss Whiley. She made some remarks about honor and tradition and gave us a summary of the proud history of the school. The school chaplain, Father Mike, started things off with a short prayer service.

Even though I had attended public school since kindergarten, my family raised me a full- fledged, card-carrying Catholic. We only attended public school because there was no parochial elementary school nearby. We did belong to St. Anthony Parish, which was five miles from home, but the parish did not have a school. My brother and I attended religion classes on Tuesday evenings at our church while we were still in elementary school. Both of us had completed the requirements for all the sacraments, and, as any good Catholics, we attended Mass every Sunday. We didn't always talk that much about God, but Brandon and I grew up knowing that faith was an important part of our lives. I never talked much about my beliefs with anyone but Jessie, so I don't know how to judge my religious status compared to others my age. But, from a very young age, I spent many days and nights praying to God about something.

The prayer service gave me a chance to catch my breath and whisper a small petition to God. But, for the last week, I doubted very much if He was listening to me.

After several more speakers, all of whom spoke mainly of school pride and academic excellence, the lights came on for a brief break. Guys made their way to the bathrooms or to the tables filled with drinks and donuts. I opened my welcome packet and slipped out the enclosed name tag. An ink pen was in the envelope too. I lifted off the cap and printed, as neatly as I could, L-E-E.

Time for a new beginning. Leo was the boy from middle school, the boy who lost his best friend, the boy who needed to forget so much in his past. Lee, the freshman, was born.

Sometime during orientation my mind and body went into cruise control. School was a comfortable place for me. The smells of new books, the hallway noises, and the anticipation of new experiences gave me a peace that I didn't know anywhere else. Yes, I liked school. Young men (the term that was repeated to us during orientation) are not supposed to admit that, but school was my safe haven. My mind honed in on that environment, and the tasks and challenges ahead enabled me to block out all the terrible things that plagued my heart.

The day went quickly, and I had some pleasant conversations with my new classmates. Even the bus ride home was an enjoyable distraction. Bus driver Joe yelled a wide variety of profanities at city motorists as he weaved and bobbed through heavy traffic and narrow streets. My mind and body ached to yell and scream too; it would be a wonderful release. But I just allowed myself the joy of listening to Joe berate the "lousy Pittsburgh drivers."

Our family dinner that evening was a barrage of questions about my day. Brandon had a weight training session and wouldn't be home for several hours. I was not used to being the center of everyone's attention, so this was difficult for me. My dad was more animated than usual. He was excited for me. I think he was relieved to have something happy to talk about with me. He repeated some of his favorite memories about being a freshmen "in the very same halls you walked in today, Leo," and he stressed the importance of school spirit and the honored reputation of North Central.

When I spoke, my voice exuded calm. I tried to sound like North Central was no big deal, but I really was excited about the new school year and the prospect of starting over.

By the end of dinner, my parents seemed content with what little I had shared. You could even see a sense of relief on my mom's face. I guess they weren't quite sure if I could adjust. I knew they still worried about my mental state.

Between the pages,
Between the ages,
A restless soul
No place to go.

—Jessie Delaney, 7th Grade

Chapter 4

THE HARRISON FAMILY high school traditions were in full swing by mid-September. My grandfather, my dad and his two brothers, and now Brandon and me, made three generations of Harrisons who attended North Central.

Brandon was going to play football this season, just because he could. It wasn't his favorite sport, but North Central had no ice hockey team. He played hockey on a privately sponsored team, but it was through my dad's urging that he signed up for football. I know my dad is really proud of Brandon's athletic abilities. Maybe more than some dads, because he was never a school athlete.

My dad is super smart. He remembers more information and details than most Jeopardy contestants. Buried somewhere in our attic are diplomas, awards, and plaques listing his academic accomplishments. North Central's school library has a Wall of Fame. My dad's name is listed among the honorees: "Wayne L. Harrison, Class Valedictorian." His job as a technology and information manager (don't ask me what he actually does) for a large computer company must pay well because my parents never complain about money. Brandon's tuition and hockey costs and now my tuition run well over ten thousand dollars a year. We live in an upper middle class neighborhood in the suburbs of Pittsburgh, and we belong to a community country club.

So, like me, Dad is more of an academician (aka, nerd) than a jock. But, since Brandon inherited my mom's family genes, he is the family sports hero. Brandon doesn't even think that running and golf (my two main activities) are real sports. "What's the point?" he would always say. "You're not really running from someone, and golf . . . well golf is just old men's hockey."

My dad took me to a golf course before I was in kindergarten. It was our special game, since Brandon found it so slow and boring. Dad is a serious golfer. But, except for the occasional instruction about my swing and my stance, he rarely talks while we're playing. We both seem to enjoy the quiet and the solitude of the game.

So, while Brandon enjoyed the Friday night football games, the screaming crowd, the cheering squad, and the marching band on display, I signed up to become part of North Central's golf team. Our practice season had actually started a little before school was in session. But, because of the events in my life at the time, my father spoke to the coach. Dad assured him that I would be ready for the team by the beginning of the school year. I went to the two-day tryout with the other guys, though, and I managed to concentrate enough to make the team.

Golf was the perfect sport for me. No spectators came to the matches. Once in a while parents would show up and follow their kid. But, since our matches were at the end of the school day (we were usually dismissed from our last two periods) few parents were able to attend.

A van picked us up in the parking lot and shuttled us, our coaches, our specially issued red golf bags, and our personal set of clubs to a golf course. We donned red polo shirts with dragon emblems and wore white North Central golf hats. We were a sports team. But, when we played, it was really one individual against the design elements of the course. It's not like football or hockey where you depend on teammates to pass or block; you alone control the outcome of your game. Of course, we did have a team score, but I could never blame anyone if my individual score was bad.

I love so many things about the game of golf. It is a genteel sport. Polite whispers and controlled conversation are an important part of the game. True golfers show love and respect for the game by following the rules and the traditions, as well as caring about the course and its natural environment.

The playing field is a beautifully manicured arena of gently rolling hills and lush greens. The chirping birds and the wind weaving among the trees are the spectators and cheerleaders. And, it is a place where, for a few hours, my heart finds rest.

The golf team became my new identity at North Central. We guys in our red golf shirts sat together at lunch and made an effort to look cool. Our conversations centered on golf or some of the other sports teams at school. That was fine with me. I needed to stay clear of any talk that was too personal. It is always hard to be a freshman, but the attachment to the golf team made school easier on many levels.

Chapter 5

ON RARE OCCASIONS, I would see Brandon in the hallways or somewhere on the campus of North Central. The physical size of the school and the big difference between the freshmen schedule and the junior schedule made contact unlikely. He would nod and give his signature eye roll to acknowledge me and then continue on with his group of most-popular-guys-on-campus.

But, we did have some daily contact. We rode the bus to school together in the mornings. Joe made numerous stops to pick up students from other schools, so the bus trip took more than half an hour. Brandon had just turned sixteen and still didn't have his driver's license, so he was probably one of the older kids on the bus and certainly one of the biggest.

There were some real lunatics on our route, but no one bothered me. On the days when I didn't have golf and was riding the bus home, I usually sat alone because Brandon stayed late for football practice. That ride was much crazier, so I usually sat near the front. Joe was big enough and sounded mean enough to have control, and I stayed close to him for some extra protection.

But, during our morning commute the bus was relatively quiet. Most of the kids went into zombie mode. One kid always looked like he just rolled out of bed, put on shoes, and sleep- walked to the bus stop. His hair was uncombed, clothes all wrinkled, and dry slobber encircled his mouth. He would plop down in the first available seat, and you could hear him snore softly for the rest of the ride. Many of the other kids were in a similar state or spent most of the time texting or looking at their phones. It was way too early for anyone to make any real trouble.

Brandon would sometimes take this quiet time as an opportunity to give me some brotherly advice. Most of his guidance came in the form of a few pointers about the classes and some information about the teachers. He had a mental list of all the things to do or avoid doing in some of my freshmen classes. He even offered to share some of his old notebooks with me.

He told me how Mr. Merlin, my history teacher, still used the same tests he designed forty years ago when teachers used typewriters and ditto machines. Merlin's test of choice was matching format, and to make it easier for him to check, he arranged the answers to make words.

The answers to one of my first quizzes in Merlin's class read down the line: F-L-I-C-K-J-A-M-B-E-D-G-H. I knew you couldn't always make words with all the letters, so I was fairly confident that I had aced the test. Sure enough, when the tests were passed back a few days later, I had a perfect paper!

Mrs. Brunline was my English teacher. Brandon was in her class his freshman year, and my Uncle Charlie had her when he was a senior.

My first day of class with her was somewhat overwhelming. Everyone said she was a demanding teacher, and her syllabus left little doubt that her standards were high. I'd never had to write any long papers before, and our course outline revealed that she expected a three- to five-page paper every two to three weeks.

Her voice was monotone and soft, and I found it very difficult to stay focused. Words were coming from her mouth, but I was just staring at her lower lip that seemed to protrude inches beyond her upper lip. She paused every few seconds seemingly to collect the saliva that accumulated in the lower reservoir of her mouth.

Behind her back, students had very easily transitioned her name to Mrs. Brunhilda. It was no great leap of the eye to understand why. She was not anywhere near attractive. Her face was slightly pockmarked and bare of any makeup. Her mostly gray hair was straight and short. Her left hand raised every few minutes and pushed some stray strands behind her ears, only bringing attention to the monstrous size of her ears. I tried to look away from her, but I was hypnotized by her odd look. She held a copy of our syllabus attached to a clipboard in her right hand. You would think that after a while the weight of the clipboard would cause her to use another hand for support. That, however, was not necessary. Her belly was so round and distended that she could literally rest the clipboard on it even though she was standing. She wore a mid-length, Mexican fiesta-looking skirt. The ruffles were having a great deal of trouble maintaining any type of smoothness as they curved around her belly. If it wasn't for the fact that she looked like she was eighty years old, most people would assume she was pregnant.

Surprisingly, she turned out to be one of my favorite teachers. She had a flare for subtle wit and an ability to inspire her class to work hard. I never adjusted my ears to listen to the monotone voice, however, and often I would need a reminder to pay attention.

"Isn't that right, Lee?" That was Mrs. Brunline's way of bringing my head back to our lesson.

"You betcha!" I would say and do my best to smile charmingly.

"Okay, that's the spirit!"

I'd like to say she smiled back at me, but those contorted lips never seemed to be able to form what looked like a smile. But I knew from the sound of her voice that I was still on her teacher's pet list. Mrs. Brunline liked me, or, more specifically, she liked my work. My papers usually were returned not only with an "Outstanding!" but also with some written notes beside things that she had circled. That's what I really looked forward to. Sure she corrected grammar and made suggestions, but she mainly commented on what she liked about my writing.

It made me think so much of Jessie and how I missed her emails and poetry. What an irony—that Mrs. Brunline reminded me of my Jessie. I guess beautiful souls come in all forms and ages.

Chapter 6

Leo, Leo,
Always be friends with me-o.

Those words were written on the tag that hung from the first Christmas present I received from Jessie—my first real present from any girl. The tag dangled from a little red and white striped gift bag. Glittery tissue paper jutted from the top.

We had just finished our short walk from the bus stop, and we were standing in her driveway. The sun was shining brightly that December afternoon, but the air was cold and damp. She leaned her backpack against her leg and reached into a side pocket. She smiled as she handed me the gift bag. "For you, Leo."

After some urging from Jessie, my hand slid the gift gently from the bag. I unfolded some more tissue paper to reveal the present. It was a blank book, a journal, with a leather-looking brown cover.

"Open it, Leo."

Inside the book jacket she had written "To Leo from Jessie. Fill this book with all the good thoughts that I know are inside your heart."

My face was turning red, and I muttered some conventional words of thanks. My mind went blank just like the book; I found it so hard to express how important that gift was to me. Rather than stand in the cold in front of her house and say nothing, I reached into my pocket and pulled out my just-in-case gift.

We hadn't said anything about exchanging Christmas gifts, but I knew if it was going to happen, it would be today. We just finished our last day of school before the long Christmas break, and I knew I wouldn't see her during those two weeks.

I had purchased the gift while my mom and I were at the mall a few weeks before. She asked me to disappear for a while. That's not-so-subtle code for "I saw something for you. So let me buy it without you seeing what it is." I took that opportunity to browse around and do some of my own shopping. I was looking for some nice, simple earrings for my mom. My dad had given me money, and he said that earrings were on her wish list.

The jewelry counter was packed with people, so I started looking at one of those little rotating stands. My eyes were drawn to a delicate silver necklace. It had a thin silver chain with a small butterfly pendant. I picked it up, and the turquoise wings seem to shimmer in rainbow hues.

I really hadn't planned on buying Jessie anything. I guess it was something seventh grade boys didn't think about. But, the necklace seemed perfect for Jessie. It would remind her of our poetry, our connection.

I managed to squeeze my way through the crowd to buy the butterfly necklace and some earrings for my mom too.

I honestly don't know if I would have had the courage to give her that gift if she hadn't handed me one. But now, that gift became an escape from my wordless, confused state.

Jessie seemed surprised that I was giving her a gift. I held it in my hand and smiled stupidly until she reached over for it. She tore off the snowflake paper and opened the box. Her hand glided over each wing as if caressing the butterfly.

"Oh, Leo," she whispered. "It is so perfect!"

Her hand went to my arm and slid down until she found my bare hand. I can't tell you how glad I was that neither of us had worn winter gloves! She squeezed my hand. If I live to be one hundred, nothing will ever top the feeling of Jessie's hand touching mine on that winter day.

Chapter 7

CHRISTMAS WAS WONDERFUL that year. My mom, Brandon, and I were on Christmas break, and Dad took vacation time. We visited cousins and good friends of the family, went to some hockey games, and of course devoured cookies, candy, and elaborate dinners.

Even with all the activity and company, I missed Jessie. I thought of her often, and we continued to share emails. To ease some of my loneliness, I would touch the leather cover of my journal and imagine the touch of her hand.

I sat at the computer most of New Year's Eve. Jessie and I sent several emails back and forth that day, and I occupied some of my time with video games.

By nine that evening, I was alone. My mom and dad went to a neighbor's party directly across the street. Brandon was at the home of one of his hockey pals, and he would be spending the night there.

Jessie and her parents were spending a quiet evening at home. Jessie quit sending emails at ten thirty that night. She said her parents wanted her to sit in the living room with them and watch the broadcast of the celebrations in New York. It was their tradition to share a little toast for the New Year.

Shortly after midnight the phone rang. Jessie's little party with her parents was already over. She was whispering, so I knew she didn't want her parents to know she was talking to me.

"Happy New Year, Leo."

"Thanks. Happy New Year to you too, Jessie."

"I was worried about you being by yourself, and of course I wanted to be the first to wish you a happy New Year."

"Did your parents give you some wine when you toasted with them?"

"Just a little, with some ginger ale mixed in. Not enough to get me drunk or sick."

I laughed at the thought of Jessie getting drunk. I was getting drunk just on the sound of her voice!

"Only two more days of vacation left." I tried to sound disgusted. "I'm going to have a hard time getting out of bed so early again. I don't think I've been up before ten, except for Christmas morning."

"Well, I can't wait to get back. I've been kinda bored. I guess life without you isn't so exciting."

My heart did a little leap at the thought that Jessie had missed me. Although I wanted to tell her that I had missed her too, the words, as usual, wouldn't come out of my mouth.

"Well, you'll probably be complaining about having too much to do after our first week back. We'll only have a few weeks left in this report card period. You know what that means—-tests, tests, and more tests."

"I'll still be glad to see you, Leo. I'd better get off the phone. Have a great new year."

She hung up so quickly that I didn't even get a chance to say goodnight. I worried that I had hurt her feelings. My hesitation in admitting how much I missed her might have upset her. I ran to my computer and hastily emailed her a message.

This email is quite messy,
But happy New Year, Jessie!
Can't wait to see your face
Just name the time and place!

It obviously wasn't my best work, but I needed to send it quickly. It was whimsical and silly, but it conveyed my feelings. I wasn't comfortable with being mushy or sounding lovesick, even though that's how I felt. I quickly hit "send." Even if she only checked her emails in the morning, she would know that I sent it right after I spoke to her.

My parents were making some noise downstairs. I went down to find them standing in the kitchen. Dad was singing "Auld Lang Syne"; he has a very good voice. They danced and hugged, and they seemed to be in the spirit of the holiday.

As soon as they saw me, they motioned me over to join them. We danced as a trio until my dad finished the song. They both kissed me and hugged me and wished me a happy New Year.

Even though they had come home only to wish me a happy New Year, they decided against going back to the party. My dad turned out the lights, and we all headed upstairs to bed.

With fingers crossed, I checked my email.

Tomorrow, two o'clock.
We'll take a walk.
Be on my street.
We'll use our feet.
We don't have to talk.

Jessie

Jessie was all bundled up in a white ski jacket. Her hair was tucked under a pink cap, and she wore pink fuzzy mittens. Her cheeks and lips were almost the same shade of pink.

She punched me playfully on the arm. "Nice poem, Leo," she said with a touch of sarcasm. "Wow, what a great rhyme . . . messy, Jessie . . . Do you realize I spent most of my early childhood trying to make sure no one ever called me Messy Jessie? I think I have OCD now because of that."

"I never called you Messy Jessie," I said in my defense. "I said my email was messy. You just don't read very carefully."

She punched me again, and then slipped her arm through mine. We walked like that for a while, and we agreed to head to the park.

The park was empty. A glaze of snow covered the ground, the trees, and the playground equipment. Jessie led the way, and I followed as I tried to mimic the patterns she designed with her boots. We made a path through trees, the parking lot, and picnic areas. We sat on the swings and smoked pretend cigarettes into the winter air. Some broken branches became our pencils as we created some silly drawings in the untouched snow that dusted the basketball court. We tried to build a snowman in the parking area, but gave up quickly because the snow was too powdery. We had a race around the baseball field until we couldn't breathe anymore. We threw snow at each other and slid down some of the small hills that dotted the park.

We stopped on the top of one of the hills, and Jessie looked at her watch. We had been out for close to an hour.

"I promised my mom I would be home to help her with dinner. So I'd better get going, Leo."

"Yeah, I promised my mom I'd be home to eat dinner."

I held my right hand above my eyes and made an exaggerated scan of the park. The once pristine snow-covered park was now totally vandalized by our footprints and artistic work. "I think our work here is done."

Jessie grinned and nodded. "Yep, we can be proud of the work we've done, and it's only the first of the year."

We left the park and walked slowly to the corner where we could see her house and where I had to turn toward my street.

"Email me later, Leo. Maybe we can do this again tomorrow." She waved her fluffy mitten playfully in my face and walked toward her house.

I just watched her for a while. "Jessie!" I had to yell because she was about sixty feet away from me. "It's already been a great New Year!"

Chapter 8

THE LATE SEPTEMBER SUN was in its glory, and the air was cool and fresh. It was the type of day that begged you to be outdoors. The North Central Junior Varsity Golf Team had a scheduled match this perfect Wednesday afternoon. The team was dismissed early, and I was grateful for not having to sit through my Algebra II and history class on a day that was made for golf.

We piled in the van and headed to a public golf course about twenty minutes from my house. It was the opposing team's home course, and many of us had played there before. Our team chatted cheerfully as we rode, and even Coach Burns was in a good mood. The air was cool and fresh, and the sun cast a golden shine on the fall foliage.

When we arrived at the course, we could hear Coach Burns on his cell talking to the coach of the team we were scheduled to play. Coach finished his call and informed us that the other team's bus never came to pick them up. They had no way of getting to the course on time, so they were forfeiting the match. We hooted and high fived because it would count as a win. Our team was not doing well, so any way we could get a win was counted as a blessing.

Coach Burns told us to divide ourselves up into foursomes. We used the day as a practice round and also spent some time on the driving range. I had one of the best rounds of my life, easily beating the other three guys. Coach Burns seemed impressed by my performance.

"That's the kind of round that shows your potential, Lee. If you stay this consistent, I can start using you on the varsity team."

"Thanks, Coach," I said. In my head I imagined my dad's expression when I shared my coach's praise.

We were done about an hour early. I knew my parents weren't going to be able to pick me up right away, and that meant a boring wait at school. So, I asked Coach Burns if the van driver could drop me off on the way back. The driver didn't need to take me all the way home; I could just get off on a main road that we had passed on the way to the match. Even with my golf bag it wouldn't be a long or difficult walk home.

The van dropped me off at a four-way intersection not even a quarter mile from my house. As the van pulled away, I waved to the guys and hoisted my golf bag over my shoulder. But I took only a few steps and then stopped. This way home was going to take me directly passed the place of the accident.

On that awful day in August, the weather had been rainy and the sky overcast. Today, the position of the early fall sun and the beautiful colors of the trees totally transformed the street.

I did have a choice. There was another street that ran parallel to this one. I would only have to walk another block down, and I could avoid this street completely.

My inner voice spoke words of encouragement; my feet did not seem as dauntless.

Hold back the tears
oh timid child
and face the fears
that your thoughtless deed has created

The street had no other pedestrians, and I slowly approached the location of the accident. Even after all these weeks, remnants of the makeshift memorial for Jessie remained. A white, wooden cross with Jessie's name printed on the crossbar was tied to the maple tree. Wilted flowers and two sad-eyed teddy bears were in the grass at the base of the tree. Colorful slips of paper with messages from friends and strangers were tacked to the trunk and low-hanging branches. Scratches, as if from a monster's claw, marred the side close to the street. They marked the place of impact after the car had swerved from the road.

I stopped several feet from the memorial and stood my golf bag up on its support legs. I pulled a Gatorade from the side pocket. I felt like a Civil War soldier taking a swig of whiskey from the flask in his saddle bag before battle. I stepped forward, knelt down in the grass, and straightened one of the teddy bears that had fallen on its side. On my knees I whispered, "I'm so sorry, Jessie. I miss you so much."

A white sports car was approaching, and I closed my eyes and wished it would veer toward the tree and hit me. Hit me and kill me so I could die just like Jessie.

The day after Jessie's death, the August sixteenth issue of the *Pittsburgh Post-Gazette* had a small three-paragraph article about the incident. It was on the second page under local news with the headline: "Young Teen Fatally Injured." According to the reporter, Jessie died instantly when hit by a car driven at the hands of a forty-six-year-old man. When the man was questioned by the police, he admitted to swerving off the road as he reached for some papers that had fallen off the passenger seat of his car. There was to be an investigation, but only minor charges were expected to be filed.

The fading motor sounds indicated that the car continued down the road. I held my eyes shut a few moments longer, trying to conjure up another car to complete my death wish. When images of Jessie's stricken body lying on the rain-soaked road filled my head, I opened my eyes.

The street was now deserted. I threw the strap of my golf bag over my shoulder and headed home. All of the joy and accomplishment of the day disappeared.

Chapter 9

WEEKS FLEW BY. The hectic school day, the golf matches, and the heavy homework load filled my weekdays. Each night I had very little trouble falling asleep as soon as my head hit the pillow. Saturday was golf day with my dad. Sunday was church with the family, and then a family dinner that included a visit from my Grandma Lily. I was thankful for all the activity because empty moments always pulled my thoughts to that day in August.

School was going well. I could find my way around campus, and my schedule was so routine that I barely checked my planner. I had a nice group of friends from the golf team. My classes were challenging and demanding.

Every week on Friday morning the freshmen class at North Central had Mass instead of our daily religion class. We walked across the campus to the chapel and sat reverently in our assigned sections. There was always perfect behavior because the principal had no tolerance for anything else. Every student knew that suspensions were often followed by expulsion from the school.

This particular October Friday we were informed that instead of Mass we would be celebrating Reconciliation. That's the fancy term for what most people call confession. Father Mike reviewed what we needed to do because he rightly suspected that most of us had not confessed for some time.

We were having a Penitential Rite. All the introductory prayers and readings would be done as a group, then individual and private confessions would be heard by Father Mike or one of four visiting priests. After completion of confessions, we would have silent reflection time and prayers of penance.

As an introduction, Father Mike read the story of the Good Shepherd leaving his ninety-nine sheep in search of the one lost lamb. He stressed how much God wanted us to be part of His holy family, and that He will always come looking for anyone who goes astray.

He walked us through an examination of conscience so that we would remember the serious sins we had committed against God and man and make a "good confession."

I knew I could not make a good confession. I could not share the serious sin that was on my soul. I could not admit to anyone, even a man of God, what I could barely admit to myself. I deserved to go to hell for what I had done; I was not worthy of forgiveness.

"I don't feel so well," I said to the guys sitting around me. I grabbed my stomach, made eye contact with Father Mike who waved me out, and made my way toward the side door of the chapel.

I sat on the steps outside with my head in my hands. When the service was over, Father Mike came over and touched me on the shoulder.

"You all right, Lee?"

"I've been better, Father."

"Report to the nurse when you feel okay to move. I'll get someone to escort you if you like."

"If you don't mind, Father, I'd like to sit here for a while. I think I'll be okay in a few minutes. I guess skipping breakfast wasn't a good idea."

If only my pain came from something as curable as eating a good breakfast. No one, especially not Father Mike, would understand how separated I was from God.

Chapter 10

JESSIE'S PARENTS, Dean and Sharon Delaney, had very little in common with my parents. Mr. Delaney was a manual laborer who worked for a home building company, and Mrs. Delaney was a part time receptionist for a large group of doctors. I don't think either one had attended college, and they didn't seem to bother too much with neighbors or school functions. They owned a beautiful home, and it was apparent that they took pride in how it looked. Mr. Delaney kept the yard neat, and Mrs. Delaney was always planting and weeding in her flower gardens.

Like my family, they belonged to our community country club, but Mr. Delaney rarely attended any events there or used the facilities. Mrs. Delaney and Jessie were often at the pool, and Mrs. Delaney belonged to some of the social clubs, including the Garden Society.

Mr. Delaney was a man of few words. Jessie said he came home from work exhausted, plopped himself down on the sofa, and watched the news until dinner. After eating, he retired to his bedroom, watched some more TV, and then went to sleep so that he could awake at five a.m. and do it all again.

On the weekends he fiddled around the house on various projects. Jessie spent time with him then. He tried to teach her how to use a hammer and screw driver. They often worked on little projects together, like building a birdhouse or making an outdoor flower planter. Anytime Jessie spoke about her father, there was a great deal of love and pride in her voice. I knew she respected his strong work ethic and was very proud of his talent for building things.

Mrs. Delaney was (and I'm using Jessie's description) a lovable but ditsy woman. She was almost five years younger than Jessie's dad and attractive when she took the time to fix herself up. She reminded me of the Charlie Brown character who always had a little zephyr of dirt around him. Mrs. Delaney often had a blouse buttoned incorrectly or wore eye shadow or lipstick hastily applied. She always looked confused or anxious. The simplest task seemed difficult for her, and she definitely was not a multitasker.

On her assigned days driving us to school, we could count on being late for our seventh grade homeroom. Halfway to school we would hear those dreaded syllables, "Oh, my . . ." Jessie and I would hold on to our backpacks and grab the edge of our seat, because those words meant a quick U-turn. We'd wait in the driveway while she ran into the house for a forgotten cell, wallet, or lunch. One time we turned around and headed back to the Delaney's because she realized that she was wearing two different shoes.

On our bus rides home Jessie would sometimes share stories about the awful dinners her mom put together. Mrs. Delaney would never quite have all the proper ingredients necessary for a recipe. In her mind, it was okay to substitute. A call for sour cream became the ranch dressing in the fridge. If baking powder was needed, baking soda was fine. And, if dinner was running late, 400 degrees for a half hour replaced 350 degrees for forty minutes.

Jessie and her father were accustomed to the food. Plus, it wasn't *always* bad, especially if she planned ahead and had the right ingredients. But every so often, when Mrs. Delaney would work on a Saturday, they would go out and enjoy lunch at a local restaurant. Jessie said she loved those moments with her dad. He had great stories about his childhood and talked extensively about politics and international affairs. Mr. Delaney was quite opinionated on many subjects, but Jessie said he encouraged her to have her own beliefs.

I'd had many conversations with Mrs. Delaney, but never really talked to Jessie's dad. Although Jessie told me he was a lovable, easy-going guy, he intimidated me. I imagined myself blubbering or going speechless in his presence. I didn't believe we had any real connection except our love for Jessie.

Chapter 11

SEVENTH GRADE WAS A GOOD YEAR for me. The stolen moments with Jessie on the bus and in the car, and the ever increasing number of emails, put me in a place of contentment and happiness. No one, including friends and family, suspected our close relationship. They knew we spent time together, but we never shared our true feelings about each other with any of our friends. Neither of us wanted to endure any teasing, and for some reason the secrecy made everything exciting and special.

Sometimes, when I would see Jessie in the cafeteria or at recess, we would catch a stolen glance. She would smile and gently lift the butterfly pendant around her neck. The gift had become a symbol of our increasing bond, and it was our own secret way of acknowledging each other in public.

After our Christmas gift exchange, the approach of Valentine's Day made me anxious. By the end of January I began to wonder about gifts and a card for Jessie. The Christmas gift was a happy accident, and I could not count on that happening again.

Our school scheduled a "Sweetheart Dance" for the seventh, eighth, and ninth grades on the Friday before Valentine's Day. Jessie hadn't said anything, and I was not quite sure how to bring up the topic. Honestly, I wasn't excited about all the silliness that goes with a teen dance, but the thought of holding Jessie in a slow dance was winning me over.

My decision ended up being made by my family. Brandon had a hockey tournament in Cleveland that whole weekend. My parents wanted us all to go and support him and his team. We would leave Friday as soon as school ended, and we would not be home until that Sunday evening.

I broke the news to Jessie on the ride home about a week before the dance.

"I really wanted to ask you to the school dance, Jessie, but my parents are making me go to Cleveland for one of Brandon's hockey tournaments."

"That's okay, Leo," she said. "I don't think my dad would let me go anyway. He says I'm too young for dates and dances. That's one of the hard parts about being an only child. Parents are pretty overprotective."

"Would he get upset if I gave you flowers?"

"Leo, you're funny! Wouldn't you look silly carrying flowers to my door. Why don't we agree to wait until the summer. You can take me for a walk and pick me some wildflowers."

That sounded great to me. And, when she squeezed my hand, I knew I had the best girlfriend in the world. We gave each other valentine cards during school hours; we had both bought each other special cards that were cute, not mushy. But she signed hers, "All my love, Jessie," and that alone made me happy.

That winter was a long, cold, snowy one. In the spring, when the days got longer and the weather got warm, everyone was eager to enjoy themselves.

Jessie joined a girls' softball league, and she was at practice or games three or four times a week. Even though she said it was her mother's idea that she play, Jessie enjoyed being around her girlfriends. I would sometimes catch part of one of her games when she played at our park. She was usually in the outfield and wasn't one of the team's best players. But she looked great in her number seven jersey and a baseball cap.

I kept busy too. I had some private golf lessons with a club pro, and I also spent time practicing at the golf range with my dad. I took swimming and diving lessons at our club's indoor pool as well.

No matter how exhausted I was after a day of school and evening activities, I always found time to check my computer for emails. We rarely let a day pass without some little note. Sometimes Jessie would send me something interesting that she found on the internet. She'd add a little note with an opinion or comment. Other times she would tell me about her softball games or something funny that happened at home.

On Sunday mornings she always sent me a poem. It became a ritual. I would awake early and get dressed for church. Then, while I waited for everyone else to rush around so we wouldn't be late for eleven o'clock Mass, I sat at my computer.

Jessie's Sunday creations were usually haikus or cinquains. They were so short and beautiful that they would instantly become part of my memory. The poems would float around in my head and become my mantras during church. Instead of praying, I would visualize her words and try to imagine what Jessie was thinking when she wrote them.

Heart beating a tune
Breath whispering the lyrics
The rhythm of life

—Jessie Delaney, 7th Grade

While my family and the other parishioners recited prayers and sang songs, I daydreamed about time with Jessie.

When Mass was over, it was time for family brunch. Sometimes we went to our club's Sunday buffet, but most often we went home. My Grandma Lily, who always attended church with us, and my mom would head directly from the car to our kitchen. Pans and dishes would clatter and bang, and within twenty minutes our kitchen counters became a breakfast buffet. Pancakes, cheese omelets, cinnamon French toast, sausage patties, orange juice, and fruit salad lined the counters.

Brandon was always first in line and would plow through, grabbing as much as he could carry. We were allowed to eat in the family room on that day. We had a bar with four bar stools, but the three guys would go right to the sofa, where we would lean over the coffee table and watch any sports thing being broadcasted that day. My grandma brought us seconds, refills, and extra napkins. She and Mom would eventually eat at the bar, but not until she knew that our every need was met. Then Mom would squeeze next to Dad, and Grandma would clean up the kitchen and clear the dishes. When everything was spic-and-span, Gram would bring out a special dessert she'd baked the night before. It was always some grand surprise; she loved trying new recipes. She would deliver an extra-large piece of cake or pie to each one of us, and then pack up and drive the fifteen minutes to her house. The four of us usually didn't move from the sofa till around three, but the rest of the day still had potential. No one needed to eat anything for dinner, and we would just do a light snack before bedtime.

I sometimes spent the late afternoon with some friends and did some male bonding. One of my friends, Jordan Kessler, was usually available to do things on Sunday afternoons. Jordan's parents were divorced, and he rarely saw his mother. His dad, Sam, was much older than mine, and he and Jordan had a somewhat strange father-son relationship. Jordan's dad treated him like an adult pal. A few times Jordan's dad even came along with him when a bunch of us were hanging out at the park.

Jordan was an easy friend for me to have though. He did most of the talking and never made any real demands on my time. He seemed content to spend time with me at a moment's notice, and I really did enjoy his company.

On the surface then, it was not apparent to our families or friends how connected Jessie and I were. Jessie spent time with other friends too. And, just like me, Jessie had some family activities going on. I think being an only child made her family demands even greater than mine. Jessie didn't even seem to have any other relatives, at least none that she spoke about.

Chapter 12

EXCEPT FOR THE HAPPY NEW YEAR CALL, Jessie and I never talked on the phone in seventh grade. Neither of us owned a cell phone then, and the family phones didn't seem private enough. We talked on the bus rides home, or sometimes we met at the park. We'd sit on the swings or walk along some of the paths and talk about a lot of serious topics. It was nice for both of us to have a conversation that wasn't focused on school gossip, sports, or television shows.

The one subject that often emerged in our talks was religion. Jessie was curious about the Catholic Church. Her parents raised her as a Christian, but they rarely attended the non-denominational church where they belonged. Mr. Delaney believed that God heard you wherever you prayed and that church was just a social event.

I couldn't argue that point. Even my mom would have agreed somewhat. But, she had always told me that praying as a group was what made going to church special.

Mom was rather opinionated about attending church. "God created us to be together . . . to work, to play, to stand together. When you belong to a group, you care. The feeling of community is very important.

It lets us become generous, giving, and loving people. Just the way God intended."

The afterlife was often a part of the religion discussions I had with Jessie. Jessie wasn't sure if she could accept the idea of heaven and hell. Sometimes her questions shook my beliefs, too.

"What if someone was raised to believe that stealing or even killing was okay? Do you remember when we read about the kids in Central America who were kidnapped from their parents and then brainwashed into fighting in a military government? How could anyone say they deserved to go to hell because of the circumstances of where they live and what they were taught to believe?"

Since I didn't have an answer, I just shrugged and changed the subject. When I got home, I asked my mom the same question.

"Well, Leo," she said with a smile, "I'm so glad you're thinking about the spiritual side of life. It's not a bad thing to question your beliefs. In fact, I think it's a necessary part of growing in faith. But to answer your question, I want you to think about what makes something wrong and sinful. An act has to be done with the intent of hurting, and secondly the person who commits the act has to know that it is wrong. I don't know about you, but I don't think children who have been brainwashed fall into those categories."

The next day I shared my mother's explanation with Jessie. Her head bobbed slowly in agreement with my mother's observation.

"That makes sense. Sometimes I think that God put evil in the world just so we can really appreciate the good things in life. I think about the idea of heaven a lot. I really don't think I'd like a place that was happy all the time. Do you think much about the afterlife, Leo?"

"Well . . ." I paused for several seconds before continuing. "I've heard of people who died and then were resuscitated. They all had a vision of a light and then saw friends and family members who had died. You know, like the people they loved were waiting for them. So I guess that's what I've always thought heaven to be. Like a big family reunion, with God as the host and hopefully the caterer too."

"Good one, Leo. Only you would still be thinking about food after you died!"

I never liked to sound too silly or insensitive when I talked to Jessie, probably because I wanted her to think of me as mature and intelligent. So, I quickly turned the discussion back to the spiritual.

"My mom has a totally different idea of heaven. She says that all heaven is, is seeing God and sharing in all his glory. She told me that God's plan is for all of us to be together. It's like a big jigsaw puzzle, but only God can see the picture it will make. When each one of us dies, we fill in the piece of the puzzle that is ours. Some people are corners and borders that frame the puzzle. Others are plain pieces, others are colorful. But, it takes all of us to make God's picture."

"You'd be a corner, Leo," she whispered. "I know you hold me together."

Jessie's email that night was titled "Heaven."

Pieces of a puzzle
Only God can see our place
His gentle hand to guide us
When we see him face to face.
The creation of a picture
So beautiful to see
As people lock together
In eternal harmony.
I really enjoyed our heavenly conversation today, Leo. I still think that you are a corner piece. What do you think I am?

Oh Jessie, I thought, I wish I could tell you that to me you are the only important piece in God's puzzle. My mind was swirling with images of Jessie's beautiful face. How much I wanted her to understand my feelings for her!

The subject of my response to her email was "Puzzle Piece."

Many pieces make a puzzle
I hold a jigsaw piece in my hand
Its edges curved in a shape that doesn't seem to fit.
It seems much too different, much too beautiful for this work.

So unique, so delicate
That I can scarcely believe it was ever in a box.
Jessie, I might be a corner, but you would be a colorful piece right in the middle! You would have no squared or sharp edges. And, I bet, in a puzzle with millions of pieces, I would still be able to find you.

Leo

Chapter 13

OUR FIRST SPRINGTIME TOGETHER went by quickly. Things blossomed, the weather stayed sunny and cool, and any moment with Jessie was magical. I was mesmerized by her beautiful smile, but our friendship now was as natural as breathing. I thought many times about kissing her, but my timing was anything but perfect. We never were alone, and I wondered if she even thought of me in a romantic way.

When the final countdown for the end of the school year began, I wondered how we could plan to see each other over summer vacation. Ever since my kindergarten years, my family did a Harrison family reunion for the entire month of July. We rented a large house at Rehoboth Beach in Delaware with my dad's brothers.

My Uncle Ken, Aunt Bev, and cousins Julie and Michael joined us there. They came from Philadelphia, and the commute was much shorter for them. My Uncle and Aunt would not stay the entire month. They left at various times to go back to work. My cousin Julie is two years younger than I, and my cousin Michael is the same age as Brandon. The cousins would stay the entire month with us and Grandma Lily. Sometimes my Uncle Charlie, who was a bachelor, would come from Richmond and stay a few weeks as well. It was a good time for the three brothers to catch up, and we all enjoyed the beach and my grandma's cooking.

On the bus ride home the first day after Memorial Day vacation, Jessie brought up the subject of summer. We had only ten days of school left for the year.

"Leo, my mom is going to take a few weeks off in June. She wants to go to Lake Erie. She thinks it will be a good 'bonding' experience for us. Then I'm staying up near the lake for two weeks of summer camp. I probably won't be home until the week of July Fourth."

Great, I thought, just days after I'll leave for Rehoboth Beach.

She went on to say that her father would only be with them for the weekends. Apparently he didn't want to take too many vacation days, and he hated the beach and swimming. He planned to stay with them for the first few days. He wanted to help them get settled and check out the rental cottage. He needed to be sure it was a safe and comfortable place for them to stay.

I pictured Mr. Delaney with his tool belt hanging from his hips. He'd check every electrical outlet to make sure it was code, look at the plumbing, and probably get on a ladder and check the roof.

Jessie saw the disappointed look on my face. I told her about our family vacation in July and said that we would be like "two ships passing in the night." She looked a little sad too, but she laughed at my reference. We didn't talk about it for the rest of the ride home.

Later, she emailed me:

Two ships passing in the night, we'll be,
One toward the lake, the other bound for sea.

In order to say our summer goodbye, we decided to meet at a little neighborhood park on the Saturday after the last day of school. It was a disgustingly humid day, and we both arrived around the same time. The park was somewhat empty because it was not even nine in the morning.

We looked like twins in our khaki shorts, our school tee shirts, and navy blue baseball hats. Jessie was sporting sun glasses, and her hair was tied back in a ponytail that stuck out from the back of the cap.

We dangled our feet in the dust as we sat on a pair of swings in a shaded section of the park.

"So, Leo, we have a bit of a conundrum here."

She wasn't just cute; she was smart. We both enjoyed words like some people enjoyed the smell of bacon. We tried to challenge each other with something like a "word of the day" game. One time we started listing the words that just sounded nice to the ears. "Onomatopoeia" was on both of our lists, as well as lots of words that were onomatopoeias, like "hush" and "buzz." She liked French words like "rendezvous" while I gravitated toward some manly words like "multiplicative."

"Hmmm," I buzzed as I made an exaggerated fingertip tap to my lips. "Perhaps we can solve this enigma by putting our Einsteinian heads together. I suggest we continue to use technology, via email, as a way of continuing our communication."

She laughed, but her expression told me she was over this game and wanted to talk seriously.

"I won't have a computer or internet, Leo. Not the whole month."

"Oh."

Then I thought about Rehoboth. My dad carried his laptop with him, but it was for business. My mom had a tablet for emails, and she used it for reading her downloaded books. I knew it would be difficult to procure their use.

My mom didn't even like us to be on any tech devices during our vacation. She wanted us to be as technology-free as possible for those four weeks. Her feeling was that we would become too easily buried in those things instead of enjoying nature and each other. She had already issued an edict stating that no Xboxes or video games were allowed. Any rainy days at the beach could be used for reading, conversing, or watching some of the PG-13 movies she thought would be enriching.

Without personal cell phones, Jessie and I had no way of communicating easily.

Jessie reached over casually and held my hand while we started to swing in sync. It felt so good, so natural, that I didn't even have time to get nervous about it. The breeze on my sticky skin and the promise of love allowed me to forget that I wouldn't see her for two months.

We stopped after an undeterminable amount of time. Jessie stood up and removed her sunglasses. She put them in her back pocket.

"I've got to go, Leo. My dad said we're leaving before lunch. I'm supposed to be packing and organizing some of the things we need to take with us. Can't trust my mom to remember everything!"

I stood up beside her. Our eyes locked, and then her hands reached out to mine. She leaned forward, closed her eyes, and kissed me right on the lips. I could feel the warmth of her skin and smell and taste her strawberry lip balm. She pulled back, and her beautiful eyes glowed lovingly at me. Then she smiled and kissed me again.

The second kiss lasted longer. She let go of my hands and turned without a word. The only thing my shocked body could do was watch as she walked away. My eyes followed her ponytail while it bounced slightly against her neck. She disappeared around a curve of the park's path.

My fingers touched my lips. How could I wait until August?

Arriving home, I ran straight to my room and shut the door. I kicked off my shoes and plopped myself on my unmade bed. I wanted to do nothing but daydream about Jessie and recreate that beautiful kiss in my mind. The heat of the day made me feel sluggish, and the house air conditioning just didn't seem to be working for me. I don't remember falling asleep, but I slept for almost two hours. It was almost noon when I awoke.

I pulled myself out of bed and straightened the covers. (I had learned early that my room could be in total chaos, but if my bed was made, my mother was happy.) I turned on my computer and saw immediately that Jessie had sent me an email.

Subject: Alien Communication

Leo,

I didn't really say goodbye because I didn't want to. Two months apart will be difficult for me. But every night at ten in the evening, I will look up at the stars and think of you. If you would do the same, I'm sure I can send my thoughts to you just as fast as an email or a phone call.

Jessie

The time stamp on the email was 10:07 a.m. Sending a reply would be a waste because they were already on the road.

Chapter 14

THE FEW WEEKS IN JUNE when Jessie was gone, and we were still home, ticked away slowly. I had plenty to do, but I missed the conversations and emails that were such an important part of my day.

My dad is big on cleaning out the garage, washing cars, and taking care of our lawn. All of those chores pretty much fell into my hands, since Brandon was usually doing some kind of ice hockey training or weight lifting. Dad did find time to get me out on our club's golf course and to the driving range. I even occasionally met some school friends at the park for a few games of wiffle ball or an attempt at tennis.

The friend I spent the most time with was Jordan Kessler. Everyone considered him weird but likable. He was at least two inches shorter than most of the boys in our class, rather average looking, but above average in the brain department. He also had more confidence than any kid I knew. Sometimes he would challenge some of the guys at the park to a tennis match or a basketball shootout. We all knew he had no chance, but he would swagger out to the court as if he were some pro athlete. After he'd get trounced (that always happened), he would give a thumbs up to his opponent and say, "Get ya next time, bro!"

He liked the girls too. Just about everyone was out of his league, except maybe the sixth grade girls. Yet again, he lacked no confidence. He would approach even a group of pretty good looking and popular girls and say something really lame.

"See any good movies lately?" or "How are you lovely ladies today?" were two of his favorite lines. He always sounded like some old dude in a '60s movie.

The girls would look at each other, shake their heads, laugh, and walk away.

He'd come back, still smiling, and say, "Their loss. Someday, when I'm a millionaire, they're gonna wish they knew me better."

I enjoyed my guy time, but that didn't stop me from missing Jessie. But I knew my time away from her would go faster if I kept busy rather than if I just sat around and moped.

My mom is off summers too, so alone time at home is rare. She likes to keep me on a good schedule during vacation days. Not too much sleeping in and not too many late nights. Usually lights were out by eleven o'clock since my dad still had to go to work in the morning.

I often just said goodnight and went up to my room around nine thirty. That gave me time to compose my thoughts. I looked up to the stars to wish sweet dreams to Jessie as soon as my digital clock blinked the ten o'clock hour. I mentally told her about my day and how much I missed her. I said a little prayer that she was safe and happy, and then I made a wish that I would dream about her.

Chapter 15

THE END OF JUNE was all about getting packed for our month at the beach. Mom was a great organizer and started filling plastic tubs with things she wanted to take. One was labeled kitchen items, another was beach supplies, and another was for games and videos. We also took bed linens, pillows, and general supplies that my mom didn't want to shop for once we got to our beach house.

Brandon and I were assigned one suitcase each and a shared bag for shoes. Luckily sandals and a few pairs of athletic shoes don't take up much space. We never bothered packing any kind of dress pants or shirt—all the churches and most of the restaurants at the beach were casual attire. It was an amazing feat to get everything into the van, even with our turtle carrier on the roof. We left just enough room for Grandma Lily and her belongings to squeeze in with us.

We left a few days early so we could spend some time at Hershey Park, Pennsylvania, on our way to Delaware. So, as our jam packed van pulled out of our driveway, it would be more than a month before we would return. Jessie was still in Erie as far as I knew. Pittsburgh faded away as we headed east along the Pennsylvania Turnpike. My thoughts drifted to Jessie's beautiful smile and, for the first time in my life, I wished that our time at the beach would pass quickly.

Our time at Hershey Park was boring for me and Brandon, and I began to think that my whole summer would be equally lame. But, our Rehoboth Beach time was great that summer. We always rented the same house because we liked the location and it had plenty of room for us, my Grandma Lily, and my Uncle Ken's family.

Brandon, me, and my two cousins were a good group. We shared similar activity levels.

Julie was somewhat of a tomboy and managed quite well in keeping up with us three guys. She was especially good at bocce ball on the beach.

My cousin Michael, my Uncle Ken, my dad, and I made a great foursome at some of the local golf courses. The four of us tried to play as much as possible. Other times were filled with swimming in the ocean, building sand castles, crabbing, or playing goofy golf. We enjoyed walking the boardwalk in the evenings. There was constant catching up on the year's events among the relatives and therefore few quiet moments.

After a few weeks, we even got to know most of the people in the neighboring houses. Sometimes my family entertained them with drinks and snacks on the huge deck of our house.

Brandon and Michael have outgoing personalities. They had befriended a group of girls and spent time with them on the beach or boardwalk every few days.

In the evenings Brandon would often meet up with one of the girls on his own. He would take a walk on the beach after dinner and wouldn't return for hours. My mom was curious, but neither she nor anyone else was getting any answers from him.

Rainy days and late evenings were for movies and board games. We watched some of my mom's picks—old movies like *Forrest Gump* and *Rudy*. My Uncle Charlie always put a little excitement into the mix by getting us more recent films, and my dad and Uncle Ken loved anything that starred Adam Sandler.

I managed to read two books that my mom had selected for me as summer reading, too. Both, of course, were books about sports.

Grandma Lily spent her days cooking and shopping for food. Aunt Bev and my mom helped with the cleanups after every meal, but both of them seemed content to let Gram be in charge of meals.

Even with all the excitement and action-filled days, there were only a few days that month when I did not remember to look up to the stars at ten in the evening. Once was when we were on the boardwalk and I didn't realize the time. On two other nights I had crashed before ten from exhaustion. But, every other night I looked up at the sky and tried to send my thoughts to Jessie. I pictured her lying on a small cot with her arms pretzeled behind her head and her eyes gazing out a window. Maybe she would just whisper, "Good night, Leo." Or, on those nights when I was alone on our beach house deck, I would hear her say, "I miss you, Leo. I love you."

July and our beach vacation rapidly ended. Dad spent much of our last few days systematically packing up our van. Our family tradition was that we needed to consume all the food in the refrigerator and have everything except two days' worth of clothes packed in the car before our last day of vacation. That would allow the last night with the family to be relaxing and enjoyable.

The last evening of our summer reunion was a feast at our favorite seafood restaurant. We reserved a private section because there were ten of us and we were a loud group. We ate lots of appetizers, and the adults toasted each other with glasses of wine. The wait staff constantly ran to our table with fried shrimp platters, crab legs, and other assorted fish. Uncle Charlie bought each of us a dessert of our choice, and Grandma Lily graciously paid for the rest of the meal.

After dinner everyone waddled out of the restaurant. My dad and two uncles ceremoniously loosened their belts as they made their way across the parking lot to our cars.

Back at the beach house we assembled on the deck for some family photos. We hugged and promised to be better about calling each other. Everyone joined in as we made a double check around the house to make sure we had all our possessions.

I pretended to join in the effort but took the opportunity to walk onto the deck. It was getting close to ten, and I was going to make my last "alien connection" with Jessie. Brandon was standing by a railing in the corner, and he looked physically ill. I figured it was because he had eaten his weight in shrimp and French fries. As I got closer to him, I could see that his tanned face had a funny ashen look, and small beads of sweat dotted his forehead.

"You okay, Brandon? You want me to get Mom or maybe a bucket for you to throw up in?"

"Not really sick . . ." He turned away as he spoke and looked out toward the ocean.

I took that as my cue to leave. But before I got far, he turned toward me and said, "I think I'm in love, Leo. I don't know what to do. There's a good chance I'll never see her again. She lives in Baltimore. Once we leave tomorrow, how am I going to deal with this?"

I didn't say anything. I just stood there thinking about how much I missed Jessie. Seven weeks without her was so difficult, and here was Brandon faced with something much worse. He would be insulted if I said I understood his pain, and there was no solution I could even offer him.

Fortunately he acted as if he didn't really expect an answer. His head shook mournfully from side to side, and he glided his hands through his sun-streaked hair.

"Don't ever fall in love, Leo. It hurts like hell."

He turned and walked down the steps to the beach. I watched as he walked barefoot along the shore, kicking sand and water every few steps. My heart hurt for him, but what could I say to make him feel better? My separation from Jessie was hard, even though I knew I would see her soon. How could anyone comfort Brandon when he had no idea how long his separation would be?

Brandon returned to the beach house about a half hour later. Michael and I were already in the room we shared with Brandon. We were packing up some of our remaining things for the morning departure. Brandon came in and grabbed a blanket and pillow from the room.

"I'm gonna crash downstairs tonight. See you guys in the morning."

As quickly as he entered, he was gone. My cousin Michael said nothing, but I suspected he knew what was going on. My sleep that night was restless to say the least. Tomorrow the separation from my love would be over, but Brandon's separation would just begin.

summer love, young love
emotions given names
no matter what the kind of love
the hurt is still the same

We left Rehoboth bright and early the next day. Brandon said he wanted to sleep and jumped right into the rear bench seat. Grandma Lily and I sat in the passenger chairs, and my mom and Dad sat in the front. A little while later we drove through McDonald's and picked up some breakfast biscuits. My mom and dad got large coffees so they could stay alert for the drive. After we were really on our way, I put my earbuds in and listened to some of my favorite music. My parents and Grandma chattered away about the month's highlights.

I was happy for the chance to daydream about my reunion with Jessie. I imagined many scenarios, all of which ended with Jessie giving me a passionate kiss.

Occasionally I looked back to check on Brandon. He was either sleeping or staring longingly out the window. Usually he spent the trip eating snacks and texting his friends, but he did none of that now.

I wondered what his girlfriend was like. I heard the name Emily mentioned the most, so I figured that was Brandon's love. Was their relationship like mine and Jessie's? My answer was no. I felt badly for Brandon, but how could anyone have the same bond that Jessie and I had? I know you can feel love for someone almost instantly, but true love happens over time. Jessie and I had something that was much more than just a physical and emotional connection. We had shared so much through our writings that our relationship was on a whole different plane. Even after almost two months of separation, my soul and her soul were one.

Chapter 16

OUR TRIP HOME turned out to be much longer than usual. Major traffic jams on the highways leaving the beach, frequent rest stops, and my mom's insistence that we stop and eat a good meal, all put us hours behind. It was after dark when we pulled into our driveway. Brandon was still rather quiet, but he seemed to be doing his best to act normally. I, however, was agitated over all the delays. I knew I couldn't call Jessie at home because at this hour her family might already be asleep. But, a quick email would work.

My mother started barking orders as soon as her foot touched the driveway. "Let's go guys. Grab some bags. I'd like to get this van unloaded right away!"

"Mommmm . . ." I said in my whiniest voice, "I'm sooo tired. Please can't I just go to bed? I promise I'll get to the van first thing tomorrow."

Brandon chimed in, "Yeah, Mom, I don't feel like doing this now either."

"Okay, guys, you don't have to whine about it. Just say goodnight to Gram, and I'll drive her home. But, I want the van emptied and clothes put away first thing after church tomorrow."

"Run, boys," my dad yelled, "before the old shrew changes her mind!" He gave one of his fake laughs to show my mom he was only kidding. We each grabbed one suitcase and made a quick beeline to our rooms.

I sat down at my desk and turned on my computer. I checked my emails, but there was nothing. Jessie probably wasn't sure I was home yet. I sat down and sent out an email to her. It was one I had composed in my head.

Subject: Return Home

Summer is almost over,
The days are growing short.
My ship has finished sailing
and entered into port.
The sky was my companion
Every long and lonely night.
But now that I have anchored
My loneliness takes flight.
For on the shore is waiting
Someone who makes my life so real
I only wish to tell her
How complete she makes me feel.

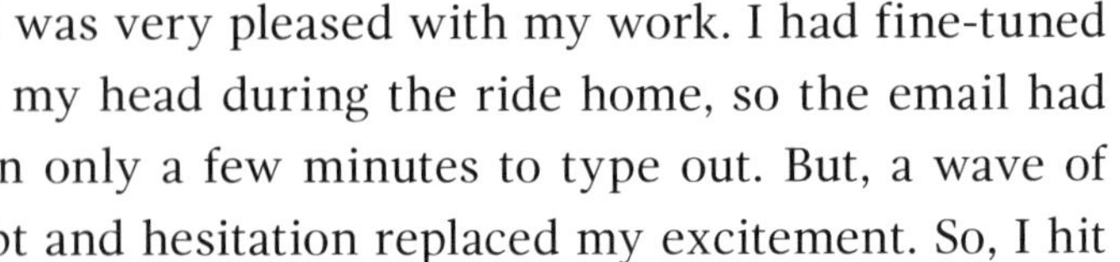

I was very pleased with my work. I had fine-tuned it in my head during the ride home, so the email had taken only a few minutes to type out. But, a wave of doubt and hesitation replaced my excitement. So, I hit "save to draft" and rewrote the email.

Jessie,

Guess Who? We're finally home after a long summer. Hope your vacation/camp experience was great. Email me back and maybe we can meet soon.

Your alien friend,
Leo

This time I hit "send." I was hoping that the reference to alien friend would remind her of our pact to look to the sky each night. I stared at the screen for a while but got no reply. I checked one more time after getting ready for bed. Still nothing. The trip wore me out, so I jumped into bed and fell asleep immediately.

The next morning I hurried out of bed before nine and went right to my computer. No email from Jessie. My friend Jordan had sent me a few emails while I was away, just short little "how ya doin'?" ones, and I responded and told him I was back home.

Everyone was up and rooting around in the kitchen by the time I went downstairs. Our pantry and refrigerator were bare after our trip, so I munched on some dry cereal. Since it was Sunday, we were headed for eleven o'clock Mass, and Dad said we'd go to breakfast at IHOP afterward. I went back up to my room and of course checked the computer again. Maybe Jessie didn't know I was home yet and wasn't even checking her emails. I thought about calling again, but that made me nervous. I was afraid that her dad would answer, and he never seemed to be very friendly.

At ten thirty we were all dressed and ready for church. Our van was still filled with things that Brandon and I had to unpack, so we took my mom's car. Church that day seemed so long, and after that we headed to IHOP. It was after two before we got home. I ran to my room, checked my email . . . nothing . . . and then changed into shorts and a tee shirt. I glanced into the mirror; I was looking pretty good! My skin was nice and tan, and I thought I looked taller and more muscular than I had before vacation. Jessie would be impressed with how handsome I had become in just a few months!

Brandon poked his head in my room. "Let's go, Leo. Mom's on me to get that car unpacked, and you're helping."

It took us at least half an hour to unpack the car. Mom made us clean out the sand and wash the bugs off the windows. We had just finished up when my mom called out to me.

"Leo, phone call."

I ran into the house and took the portable phone from my mom. I stepped out onto our back patio for some privacy.

"Hello?" I felt my stomach suddenly churning with nervousness.

"Hey there, Leo. Glad you're back from the beach."

It was Jordan, not Jessie. He wanted to shoot some basketball at the park. My heart wasn't in it, but I said I'd meet him in an hour. My plan was to take the long way to the park so I could walk by the Delaney's house. If there wasn't a car in the driveway, maybe they were away on another trip. It was the only possible reason why Jessie hadn't answered my emails.

I freshened up and then told my parents I was headed to the park. They were going food shopping and told me to be back by seven so that we could eat dinner together.

The walk to Jessie's was only about five minutes. My head was spinning with worry about why she hadn't responded to me yet. I turned the bend and stood behind a tree across the street from her house. On the driveway was her mom's car. Jessie's dad usually parked his truck in the garage. Chances were good that they were home. I watched the windows and the side porch to see if there was any activity. I decided to wait by the tree for a while; I still had fifteen minutes before I was to meet Jordan.

After a short time, the Delaney's front door opened. Mrs. Delaney emerged and headed for her car. Seconds later, I spied Jessie standing at the doorway. My heart did flip-flops. She looked so beautiful. Her brown hair was streaked with light shades of blonde from the summer sun, and she looked so mature. I couldn't help but notice that she had a more womanly figure.

Instead of shouting out to her, I watched as she got into the car with her mom. I hid behind the tree and didn't move until the car was around the next block.

What was my problem? Why didn't I yell out to her? Well, at least I knew she was home. Now the only question was: Why hadn't she answered my emails?

Jordan was waiting at the basketball court by the time I arrived at the park. We talked a little about things we had done during the summer. We played some man-on-man for about fifteen minutes and then sat down to take a breather.

"So, Leo, have you seen your friend Jessie lately? I saw her and her mom last week when I was at the pool, and va-va-va-voom, if ya know what I mean!"

I turned away and dribbled the basketball between my legs as I sat on the bench. My face felt drained of color, and I felt embarrassed and upset over Jordan's comments. I just muttered something about how I haven't seen anyone because we got back from vacation just last night.

"Well, I tried to talk to Jessie a little at the pool. She had her head buried in a book and didn't seem too friendly. I guess now she thinks she's too hot for boys her own age. Her mom was with her, and she even seemed embarrassed because Jessie wasn't talking much. I overheard Mrs. Delaney tell my mom that Jessie was always reading and spending too much time on her computer at home. Almost like she was making excuses for Jessie being so rude."

I felt physically sick at this point. Apparently there was no logical reason why Jessie wasn't returning my emails. She was home, and her computer worked. The only reason left was that Jessie was done with our friendship. She was out of my league now, and all my dreams of romance and love were just that . . . dreams!

I looked at my watch, and even though I had time, I told Jordan I needed to head home for dinner. Jordan said he was going to stay longer, and he picked up the basketball and started shooting. I walked away until I got to a wooded area. After making sure no one was around, I leaned against a tree, put my hands on my face, and cried like a baby. Brandon's words echoed in my ears. "Love hurts like hell."

At dinner that night everyone at the table was pretty quiet. We were tired from yesterday's long trip and all the busy confusion of today. No one noticed my mood or asked me any questions about Jordan. My dad had to get up early for work the next day, so by nine o'clock we all were in our respective bedrooms and ready to call it a day.

I was under my covers by nine forty-five, and the only light in my room came from my Star Wars night light and my computer screen. My monitor beckoned me, but I wasn't up for any more disappointment today. "Think of something else," my mind was telling me. I tried to conjure up a vision of the beach and the relaxing sounds of ocean waves. When I opened my eyes again, I averted them from the computer screen.

They landed on my digital alarm clock just as it flashed 10:00. I slipped out of my bed and looked out of my window. "Good night, Jessie," I whispered to the sky. "No matter what, I'll always love you." My voice broke as I said those words, and I felt another refrain of tears coming on.

The first thing in the morning and many times in the next few days, I checked my email. Disappointment was eating away at me. Eventually, I just stopped. Jessie no longer considered me a friend. She had out-grown our relationship.

August that year was hot, muggy, and unbearable. The guys and I spent most of our afternoons at the pool, but no one wanted to be outside any other times. Occasionally, Jordan came to the house, and we watched a video or played Xbox. My mom was occupied with getting things together for a new school year, and Brandon was back to hockey practices and weight training. Dad was busy working, and even he thought it was too hot to play golf or grill outside.

The third week of August brought daily thunderstorms to the area. It rained almost constantly; the news talked about flooding in local river towns.

Our neighborhood yards looked like jungles, and I felt trapped and depressed. I had eaten almost every piece of junk food in our pantry, and there was not one television show, movie, book, or video game that held my interest. I avoided even looking at my computer, but I longed to write to Jessie. Sometimes I curled up on my bed in the middle of the afternoon and took a nap so I could daydream about her.

I had a hard time conjuring up a picture of her face. Had all her physical changes really changed what was inside? I remembered her butterfly poem and wondered if the old Jessie had been the caterpillar. Maybe now that she had transformed into a butterfly, she was flying away from me forever.

The misery of August seemed to last forever, and then suddenly the storms ended, the weather cooled dramatically, and the smell and the noises in the air hinted that autumn was nearby.

My mom dragged me to the mall, where we bought school clothes. A backpack, notebooks, pens, and a scientific calculator were purchased too. The only real excitement I felt was when my parents surprised me with a cell phone. They finally agreed that it was necessary at my age. They just made me agree to some restrictions. Mom said the cell would be confiscated if I used it late at night or during any of my classes. I was also to report immediately if I received any inappropriate messages or pictures from anyone.

My parents believed I was totally ready for the school year. I had the clothes, the phone, and the school supplies. I didn't feel prepared at all.

Chapter 17

BRANDON STARTED BACK TO SCHOOL before Labor Day. My mom had in-service days to attend in preparation for her school opening the Tuesday after Labor Day. So, I had a few days at home alone—something very rare in the Harrison house. I was determined not to waste the time feeling sorry for myself, so I invited Jordan over. We quickly grew bored of video games, and I got frustrated playing catch and badminton with Jordan in our back yard. Jordan could rarely catch a ball or return a birdie. He is not athletic, but he is inventive.

At Jordan's suggestion, we went to my room and collected some of the Star Wars figures from my bookcase. The whole series of Star Wars movies are my favorite things to watch. I'm not a big collector in general, but I have a respectable collection of Star War figures and cards.

Jordan went to my closet and pulled some shoelaces from my shoes. He stood on my desk chair in the middle of my bedroom and tied a lace to each of the five blades of my ceiling fan. He then tied the hanging piece of the lace around the necks of Han Solo, Luke Skywalker, Darth Vader, Chewbacca, and Princess Leah. Each figure hung from the ceiling fan at about waist level.

I slid my desk chair out of the way, and we each grabbed one of my lightsabers. Then Jordan flicked on the fan. As the Star War characters flew in circles around the middle of the room, we made exaggerated moves with our sabers and fought our way across the room. We dived off my bed and fought our way back. Jordan made saber noises and rolled on the floor, feigning injury. I held my lightsaber in one hand in order to hold away the attacking figures swinging overhead, and I used the other hand to drag Jordan to safety.

But, it was really Jordan who rescued me. I laughed for the first time in weeks, and it felt so good. Maybe, just maybe, I would survive the heartbreak of a lost love.

After an activity-filled holiday weekend, the tension about the new school year returned. Labor Day marked the end of summer and the beginning of eighth grade. I wasn't uneasy about school, but I was troubled about seeing Jessie.

Under the covers, with my hands crossed behind my head, I stared at the ceiling of my room. Small shadows formed images of a school of fish. Snapshots of the ocean waves and sandy beaches flashed in my brain. I thought about all the highs and lows of the summer. Then, as my mother taught me, I thanked God for everything.

I continued with a whispered prayer: "Lord, you know the pain that's in my heart. If Jessie won't ever love me, let me learn to deal with it. Let me be able to find joy in other things. Amen."

Strangely, I could not ask God to help me stop loving Jessie. I wanted to keep loving her, even though it hurt. Even the hurt was better than emptiness.

I heard everyone moving around the next morning about fifteen minutes before my alarm was set. As soon as I awoke, a feeling of dread filled my stomach. My breathing became rapid, and my hands started to shake. I felt all of my courage and confidence fly out of my body.

Jordan had agreed to come to my house, and then we would walk to our bus stop together. Jordan assumed that this was because we were now best buds, but I had a different reason. Two bus stops from mine was Jessie's. With Jordan sitting beside me, I could talk to him and have some feeling of security when Jessie got on board. Even with this added security, I still didn't know what my reaction, or for that matter, what Jessie's reaction would be. She had not seen me since June. I regretted that my tan had faded and worried that I would look like an immature dork to her. Or, even worse, I worried that she would not even look my way.

My alarm blasted, and I hit it hard. My feet slowly edged out from the covers and onto the floor. "Suck it up, Leo," my inner voice echoed as I went about my morning routine.

Brandon was already gone by the time I got downstairs to the kitchen. His bus to North Central left before I even got out of bed. Dad was gone too. My mom was still upstairs, so I had a few minutes to compose myself. I grabbed a bowl, filled it with cereal and milk, and sat at the kitchen island to eat. Glancing at the clock, I saw I had ten minutes before Jordan arrived. I finished my cereal and went back to my room to grab my backpack. Mom was just coming out of her room.

"Give me a hug, Leo." She opened up her arms, and I was there in a second. She squeezed me tightly and kissed my cheek. "You are getting so tall and handsome. All the girls will go crazy over you now that you're such a tall, good-lookin' eighth grader! Have a great day and a great school year, sweetie."

"Thanks, Mom." I really meant that, too. Sometimes a hug from Mom just eases the pain. And, even though her words about my looks were biased, they did help build my confidence. I grabbed my backpack, told Mom I was going, and headed out the door.

Jordan was walking up our driveway. His grin revealed that he was obviously excited about getting back to school.

"Let's get goin', Leo. I can't wait to boss around those seventh graders. This is going to be the best year ever!"

We stood at the bus stop for a good ten minutes before the bus arrived. Only about ten kids were already on it. Jordan and I nodded hello to some of them and then found a seat close to the back. Now that we were eighth graders, the back of the bus belonged to us and the ninth graders.

As soon as I sat down, that awful feeling of dread returned. I sat by the window; I needed to be able to look away when Jessie boarded.

Two stops later, Jessie stepped onto the bus. Her hair still glowed with summer highlights and was cut in a new shoulder-length style that framed her face. She looked like a high school girl, and her navy blouse and patterned mini-skirt accentuated her newly developed figure. I swear everyone on the bus stopped and stared at her. She locked eyes quickly with her friend Katie who sat toward the middle of the bus. She didn't smile or wave at anyone. She just sat on the aisle seat next to her friend and then disappeared from my view.

"See, that's what I told ya, Leo," Jordan had that same excited grin on his face. "Jessie is really hot! I guess she knows it, too, because she didn't even give us a nod. I always thought you two were good friends. Didn't you use to ride to school with her in the morning?"

Even though I wanted to smack the grin off Jordan's face, I tried to stay calm. "Her mom and my mom go to work earlier this year, so we have to take the bus now." That was true, but it didn't really tell the whole story. I definitely wasn't up to explaining how Jessie didn't even respond to my emails or how hurt I was that she just threw our friendship aside.

"Yea, I guess she thinks she's too good for all of us now."

Before Jordan could press me any further, I steered the conversation towards what classes we would have together. Jordan talked about how excited he was about his classes, and I turned my head toward the window.

"Please, God, let me get through this," I mumbled to the window.

Our middle school building approached, and the bus entered the parking area, circled around the back of the building, and then stopped in line behind a few other buses. There were lots of kids milling around the front of the building. We all looked brand new—new haircuts, new clothes, new shoes, new backpacks. Amazingly, in a few days all that crispy, neat look would disappear, and the real look of middle schoolers would emerge. Disheveled hair, sloppy jeans, dirty shoes, and backpacks bulging with books and stained with God-knows-what, would replace this wormhole in time.

Before our bus even come to a stop, everyone was getting up, grabbing backpacks, and working their way down the aisle. Jordan was one of the first to his feet and quickly scooted forward. Jessie was one person in front of him. In his cool-dude style, he shouted to her.

"Lookin' good there, Jessie. Hope we have some classes together."

Jessie turned around, and her face looked either embarrassed or upset. She gave him a little hand wave and continued down the aisle. In those brief seconds she had looked me in the eye. I guess the little wave was for me and Jordan. There was no longer any doubt in my mind that Jessie didn't want anything to do with me.

We always got our homeroom assignments and our schedules in the mail about a month before school started, so I knew exactly where to head when I got into the building. Jordan and I were in the same homeroom, and we also had American History together. I was praying that Jessie wasn't in any of my classes. How could I bear being so physically close to her every day?

Our homeroom teacher told us that, for the first day, we were running an entire schedule, but each class would only be twenty minutes long. We were having extra homeroom time to go over some procedures, get our locker assignments, and review basic school behavior rules and policies. We would have a regular lunch schedule, and then at the end of the day, there was a school assembly.

I managed to get through the morning and through lunch without any Jessie sightings. My first period after lunch was Algebra I. It was an advanced class, so it was small. Miss Parker gave us assigned seats, and I ended up sitting beside Katie, one of Jessie's friends.

"Hey, Leo, glad to see you're in this class. We're lucky to get Miss Parker. She doesn't usually give too much homework, and she's a lot nicer than Mr. Santucci."

"Yeah, I heard that too."

"Jessie just asked me at lunch if I had any classes with you. Have you talked to her lately?"

My pulse quickened at the thought of Jessie asking about me. I tried to keep my voice calm and cool. "Nah, I've been away most of the summer so I haven't seen too many people. Jordan is about the only person I've talked to."

"Well, . . . don't say anything, but Jessie seems different . . . I don't know. She's been really quiet. She hardly said anything on the bus this morning. I called her a few times last week . . . ya know, just to compare schedules and see how her summer went. Her mom kept making excuses for her, but I know she just wouldn't come to the phone. She talked a little more at lunch with all the girls, so maybe it's just me."

Before I could ask any questions or probe Katie for more information, Miss Parker asked for quiet and started going over expectations for the year. It's a good thing she had all that information written down on a handout for us. All I could think about was what Katie had said. I was relieved that Jessie had rejected others, not just me, but I was worried about what she might be going through.

When class was over, Katie ran up to Miss Parker to ask her something and, I guess, get some brownie points early in the year. I made my way into the hall and to my last class of the day. It was in the room across the hall. About half the class was headed there too, and we had our pick of seats. We all headed to the back of the room. Our instructor, Mrs. Warren, entered the room and pointed to the board.

"Check your schedules," she began, "and make sure you are assigned to a double period of advanced Language Arts with me."

She stood by the door and greeted the students who were just coming in and repeated her direction about checking schedules several more times. I sat next to Matt Gavin, who was a real math whiz. We had known each other since kindergarten and had spent some time together at the pool in the past.

Matt was one of those guys that have it all. He was tall, good looking, smart, and as if that wasn't enough, he was nice too. He was a real chick magnet and had already had a few serious relationships during middle school. He was the captain of our school basketball team, and he had star-quality written all over him.

We talked about some of the weird teachers we'd had over the years, and he started imitating Mr. Conway, our second grade teacher. Matt had Mr. Conway's speech flaws down perfectly.

"Now, Weo, pwease wet the cwass know how wong a meter is."

Matt kept going, and I was laughing pretty loud. Mrs. Warren corrected us from the doorway. "Let's hold it down, gentlemen. Your time would be better served reviewing the contents of your literature books."

She drew my attention to the door just as Jessie entered the room. Again, our eyes met. This time she gave me a half smile and a slight nod of her head. Then she slid into a seat at the very front of the room, set her books on the desk, and opened up a notebook and began writing. It was obvious to me that she was giving off a signal: don't bother me.

"Oh, Jessie," I thought, "what has changed you?"

I wanted so badly to move next to her and just touch her shoulder. Something told me that she was hurting, but what could I do? That beautiful sparkle in her eyes was gone.

If love alone could heal your heart
My love would ease your pain.
But you have closed the door to me
Outside I will remain.

The day ended with a school assembly. All the teachers were introduced, and then there was a brief fashion show demonstrating what was considered appropriate school attire. After that, various organization leaders spoke to recruit for their groups. The school activities committee (which included working in the concession stand) said that they needed more volunteers. I wondered if Jessie would sign up again.

I decided it didn't matter; I needed to live my life. Jordan and I agreed that we would sign up for the activities committee, and I also signed up for intramural track. I left some other options open because we still had several weeks left to decide.

Mom's car was in the driveway when I got home, but I managed to avoid her and get to my room. I wasn't in the mood for questions about my day. After putting on some comfortable clothes and emptying my backpack, I was ready to go and enjoy the rest of the day. Dinner wasn't until seven o'clock, so Jordan and I were going to the park. I texted him that I was on my way, yelled to Mom where I was going, and scooted out the door before she could stop me.

Again, I used the excuse of a trip to the park to walk past Jessie's house. Jessie was not on the bus after school today, and I guess I just wondered if she was home. I tried to walk casually, but at the same time, I tried not to be seen. No cars were in the driveway, and there was no sign of activity. I continued on and met Jordan at the park.

Dinner was already prepared when I got home. We were eating on the deck. Mom had everything lined up in the kitchen, so we just filled up a plate and made our way outside.

"So, Leo, any schedule mess-ups this year?" My dad posed that question and then focused his attention to the pile of lasagna, garlic bread, and broccoli on his plate. He was referring to the embarrassment I endured my first year in the middle school building. Somehow (to this day, I think Brandon had something to do with it) all of my information was tagged for Leona Harrison. Teachers had me on their roster that way, so any time they took roll that first day, they would call out for Leona. Everyone in my class would giggle and point.

"She's over there," some jerk would always say.

The worst part was when I had to report to the girls' gym class and explain that I didn't belong there. Of course, I also had to endure being called Leona by my classmates for about two weeks.

"No, Dad. No gender confusion with me this year," I snapped back.

He spat out some of his garlic bread when he couldn't control his laugh. My dad loves a good play on words, and I was proud to be able to make him laugh.

We had a nice dinner and watched the sun go down as we enjoyed a dish of ice cream and a chocolate chip cookie.

Everyone pitched in with dishes, and we watched some TV in the family room. I showered and did the short algebra review page we were assigned and then jumped into bed. I was tired, but a barrage of thoughts made me restless. I remembered Jessie's sad eyes—she had lost that bottomless chasm of happiness that had defined her. I mentally began a list of possibilities that could have changed her so much.

1. Her mom and dad were getting divorced. This seemed somewhat likely to me since I had never witnessed any type of amorous display from them. Of course, I had not really seen them together much either, and that added to the divorce theory.

2. Her mom or dad was really sick, like with cancer or something. When I was in fifth grade, my friend Thad's mom was diagnosed with cancer. She was in and out of hospitals every few weeks, and he would start crying in class because he was so worried. She died at the end of the school year, and he and his dad moved

somewhere else. A family illness would explain her sadness, but no one looked ill.

3. She had fallen in love with someone else over the summer, maybe while she was away. Either he didn't love her back, or she was upset because she couldn't see him anymore. I thought about Brandon and his summer love.

Of all these options, I was hoping it might be the divorce. I figured eventually she would learn to accept her parents' getting divorced. After all, half of my class was in a step family or single-parent home. The only worry I had was that a split might mean she would move.

Then I felt so bad over my selfish, even cruel, thoughts that I added another reason to the mental list:

4. You are such a selfish, unworthy person that Jessie never wants to see you again. She looks sad because she can't figure out what she loved about you in the first place.

Chapter 18

AFTER ONLY A FEW WEEKS into my eighth grade year, I was shifting back into my comfort zone. The school routine had kicked in, and everything except my relationship with Jessie was on a normal track.

Jordan and I hung out together most of the time, but I had a wide group of friends—including some girls—that I felt comfortable around. My school day was becoming more bearable because I knew that there were only two times I had to see Jessie: on the morning bus and during my last double period of Language Arts. Jordan was always my buffer in the morning, and our Language Arts class had twenty-two students. Jessie was rarely on the afternoon bus, so that part of my afternoon was simple.

Despite my agreement with Jordan, I decided against signing up for the school activities committee. I didn't want to chance being around Jessie, and truthfully I had lost interest in the committee. Instead, I summoned up some courage to run for student council.

Only the ninth graders were allowed to run for president and vice president (not that I would have considered either), but all other positions were open to any grade. I decided to run for class representative. I only had to be elected by my homeroom, and then I would just attend student council meetings and report information back to my class.

Elections were held during the last week in September, and I beat out two of my classmates. That simple little election built up some of my confidence. I felt less like a loner and more like one of the popular kids.

I also signed up for intramural track and the golf club. With track, it was basically a fitness thing. Our sponsor kept a log of our times and how much we were improving. Once in a while we competed with other schools, but we had no real schedule of meets.

We didn't have an eighth grade golf team, so golf club was just a bunch of us who would do outings together under the supervision of a teacher or volunteer parent. We either played nine holes or practiced at the driving range and putting greens. Golf club was mostly an early fall and spring activity. But, since there were many indoor driving ranges in the area, we also practiced in January and February.

My parents were pleased with my activities. They always stressed with me and Brandon the importance of having a well-rounded school résumé. Most universities expected a wide range of extracurricular activities along with good grades.

Jessie was in none of my activities. I told myself that I was moving on, but my heart knew better. Everything I did was dependent on Jessie. If I didn't care, I wouldn't have even considered her in the equation.

My clothes were chosen to impress her; my activities were chosen to avoid her. I wondered what she was doing and who was with her. I tried to make her jealous by hanging out with other girls, and I hid the fact that I missed her. I was not moving on, but I hoped I fooled her into thinking I had.

The academic part of the school year was going well. The teachers were challenging without being too demanding; I had a lot of homework, but nothing I couldn't handle. The only class that was boring was my history class, and my favorite class by far was Algebra. Language Arts would have probably come in second, but Jessie's presence made me feel anxious.

In Language Arts, Mrs. Warren told us we could select our own seats as long as we behaved. Jessie sat in the front and didn't really socialize with many people in the class. I was in the back with Matt and a few of his friends.

Since this was an advanced class, we were all serious students. We had a double period because we needed to cover literature, English grammar, writing, and vocabulary. I liked our literature book, which was full of short stories and poetry, and Mrs. Warren allowed the class to vote on a novel to read each quarter.

Our class time was usually divided into some English grammar practice, some oral reading and discussion, silent reading, and writing. We had laptops available in class to do research and to type writing assignments.

Since I was across the hallway the period before Language Arts, I always got settled in before Jessie arrived. When class was over, I made sure she left before me. In between, we had very little contact. Sometimes, however, especially during silent reading, I would try to steal a look at her. Just as with most of the other times in class, she looked distant and sad.

When I would catch a glimpse of her in the hallways or the cafeteria, she was more animated and seemed to be enjoying the company of her other friends. I wasn't sure what conclusion to draw from this, but it made me think that I was the only person she had an issue with. Her friend Katie never mentioned her concern about Jessie's behavior again, and I was reluctant to bring up the subject.

At times she would give me a brief wave, or even say hello, but we certainly didn't share any moments together.

At home, my computer constantly reminded me of Jessie, but I used it anyway, mostly for school assignments. One or two emails from friends arrived occasionally, but I stopped even hoping for one from Jessie.

Our second quarter ended in the beginning of November, and I made high honor. I had been pushing for all As, but a B in history and one in Algebra spoiled my effort. Our names were posted on the hallway bulletin board, and I noticed that Jessie also made high honor.

We started a new novel in Mrs. Warren's class. The class had selected *Witness* by Karen Hesse. It is a historical novel that focuses on racism in a small rural town in Vermont in 1924. It is written in free verse, and since most of us had read *Out of the Dust*, also by Hesse and written in the same style, we thought it was a good choice.

Even though it was an easy, quick read, there is so much symbolism and so many historical references in the book, we spent four weeks reading and exploring *Witness*. We had many quizzes on our readings in those weeks, but Mrs. Warren wanted us to do something different when we completed the novel. She asked us to do some type of oral presentation that had to do with the book. She suggested doing a memorized reading of one of the characters' parts, a speech about racism, or a presentation of an original writing in a style similar to Hesse's.

We had a week to prepare, and then it would take about three days to do the twenty-two individual presentations. I never liked to stand in front of class, so my plan was to do something short. Our evaluation depended on our delivery (eye contact, voice projection, proper inflection), so Mrs. Warren allowed us class time to practice with a partner.

I decided to do a recitation of one of the character's parts. Most of the good characters are female, and I didn't want to imitate their voices, so I chose Johnny Reeves, the pastor who is both a hypocrite and a racist. I DVR'd some preachers on Sunday morning television to get that fire and brimstone inflection and spent time rehearsing in front of my bedroom mirror.

Mrs. Warren randomly chose the order for our presentation. I was number fifteen, almost toward the end. I had hoped for an earlier position just to get it over and done. Being fifteenth just meant more time to worry myself about it.

We were in our second day of presentations, and very few of them were outstanding. Some were just awful.

Matt was called to present. We had the choice of using a podium or not, and most people chose the podium for support. Matt, being Matt, did not need any support. He chose to perform the part of Esther Hirsh, an innocent and sensitive six-year-old girl. Matt used some props—a curly wig and an apron. (He said he was too manly to perform in a full dress.) He used a voice that was squeaky and childish, and a half hillbilly, half New York accent.

" . . . .whose poor head did have a bullet inside it . . . .daddy said that bullets are a very bad thing . . . you can even get a shooting in the head and still be okay . . . ."

He had to start over twice because the class was laughing so hard, but Matt managed to stay in character. He put us all to shame, and Mrs. Warren applauded his effort and talent.

Two presentations later, I was up. I chose to use the podium for support; my knees shook the entire time. In the character of Johnny Reeves, I did a fairly good rendering of a preacher's voice. I slipped up only once and had to be cued by Mrs. Warren.

During the presentation I looked at the back wall of the room. I was too nervous to make eye contact with anyone. But, when I was finished, I looked over at Jessie. She had a little smile on her face, and I heard her whisper, "Good job, Leo," as I passed her desk.

My knees continued shaking for about five minutes after I sat down. Matt slapped me on the back and said, "Noble effort, young man." That was a favorite saying of our history teacher, and I gave him a sarcastic "thanks a lot" in return.

By the third day, most of the class had completed their presentations. Only four people were left, and Jessie was called first. She carried a few sheets of paper with her and walked to the podium. Her hair was getting long again, and she wore a soft cream-colored sweater and a brown skirt. She smiled at everyone, and her green eyes sparkled.

"I've chosen to do an original writing in response to our novel. I tried to imagine what it was like to be Leanora Sutter, only twelve years old, and having to face the isolation and the hatred she faced. How difficult it must have been for her and her father to be the only black people in a town in Vermont in 1924. Even her father referred to her as a "wild brown island."

She cleared her throat and sighed softly. Her hands held the paper steady. When she finally spoke, her voice was strong and powerful.

Am I an island?
Not by my own choosin'
an island I've become.
Ain't it bad enough to be twelve
Tryin' to figure out who I am and where I'm headed?
Don't see no future here
White people don't see my soul
they don't see my heart.
they don't see me cryin' alone in my room
a weed in their perfect garden
a worm in their apple.
If I could find an open door
I would enter
So thirsty and hungry am I
No hesitation, no looking back
I would just walk right in
Here I am
Just a person
Not an island
Just a person.

The class was quiet for a while as Mrs. Warren praised Jessie for doing such a good presentation. She had complimented most of us, but Mrs. Warren also asked Jessie if she could give everyone in the class a copy of her presentation.

"Jessie, you did a wonderful job, but I think we all need a hard copy to really appreciate your hard work."

The praise seemed to touch Jessie, and for the first time in a long while, she had a full smile on her face.

She made her way to her seat, and many people in the class made positive comments and congratulated her.

After the last three presentations, there was less than ten minutes left in class. Mrs. Warren commended us on our work and told us to enjoy our weekend. She gave us the remaining time just to relax and talk quietly.

Some people got up and moved around, others stuffed books and papers away, and a few students made their way to Mrs. Warren's desk to ask questions about their grades.

When I spied an empty desk beside Jessie, I went up and sat beside her. She stopped writing in her planner, looked over at me, and smiled.

"Your presentation was really great, Jessie. You always impress everyone with your writing."

"Thanks, Leo. You did a good job too."

"I just recited—you recited and wrote yours. I can't compete with that."

She reached over and put her hand on top of mine. "Don't ever doubt your writing skills, Leo. You can compete with anyone. I wish . . . ."

Just then the bell rang, and the commotion of students sliding chairs and making a way for the door halted Jessie's words in midair. I guess she took it as a sign to stop talking. She removed her hand and smiled at me.

"Have a great weekend, Leo." She grabbed her books and disappeared into the hallway.

Chapter 19

The weekend seemed dreadfully long. I spent Friday night playing Xbox with Jordan. For most of Saturday we were at the hockey rink watching Brandon's team. Sunday morning was church, and the rest of that day we ate and watched football games.

All the time I wondered about Jessie. That moment on Friday felt so good. She connected with me for the first time since June. I started checking my email again—every few hours—with the hope that she would contact me.

When my alarm buzzed on Monday morning, my dreams turned back into doubt. Friday's elation waned, and I began to think that I had imagined any reconnection with Jessie.

As usual, Jordan and I sat together on the bus. He was excited about an old black and white film he and his dad watched on Sunday night. He began a wordy summary along with some impersonations of the actors and actresses in their parts.

A light snow fell outside and a hazy mist hung low in the air. The bus windows clouded over and the air was damp and cold. Even though I knew it was Jessie standing at her bus stop, I could barely see her. The hood of her charcoal gray coat was pulled over her head, and her hands were stuffed into her pockets.

My heart sank with the anticipation that she would slide into her seat next to Katie and be oblivious to my presence. Even worse, I worried that she would give me a sad, blank stare as if I didn't exist.

Jessie walked up to the last step into the bus, removed her hands from her pocket, and brushed some snow from her hood. She pulled the hood back and stepped into the aisle. Instead of looking toward her usual seat, she looked towards me. Our eyes met, and she smiled. It was a real smile, one that lit up her whole face, and I could see my old Jessie inside. I smiled in return, and Jessie slid quickly into her seat as the bus jerked back into motion.

". . . yeah, Leo, the action scenes were pretty funny. Guys were getting shot, and they didn't even show any blood! My dad said that when he was little . . ."

Jordan's voice entered the twilight zone of my mind. The only thing that mattered was the little miracle I had just witnessed.

After the bus came to its final stop at school, everyone moved with the typical disorganization of unloading. Kids put coats back on, grabbed backpacks, put away their cells, and moved at a rate that showed no desire to get into the school building.

As I collected my things, my mind debated my next move. Should I play this cool, or should I rush up to Jessie and try to talk to her?

Jordan had me corralled into my seat as he fumbled with his coat. His jacket sleeve was twisted with his backpack. Jordan and his whole mess blocked my exit. It took a lot of self-control for me not to push him aside. I looked up as Jessie got in the aisle. She gave me a quick wave.

"See ya later, Leo!" She smiled and disappeared into the crowd.

All day my eyes scanned the hallways and spied into classrooms with open doors. But, I didn't see Jessie again until Language Arts. I watched from my seat in the back of the classroom as she entered the room. She caught my eye before she got into her usual seat. Her eyes lit up again with a slight smile.

It was a three-day school week, since Thanksgiving was Thursday. School would resume Tuesday. That short holiday week made me feel optimistic and hopeful. Every day, Jessie greeted me on the bus and at the beginning of Language Arts class. We didn't have any real conversations, but there was a glimmer of friendship and caring in her eyes.

On Wednesday she waited for me after class.

"Have a good Thanksgiving, Leo. Say hello to your mom for me, too. I miss our rides to school in the morning."

"Thanks. We're going to make a trip to Ohio to see my grandparents from Thursday to Sunday."

"Hope the weather is good for your trip. They're calling for some snow on Saturday."

"What are you doing for Thanksgiving?" I was trying to keep this conversation going, even though we were both headed to the hallway. We'd soon have to split and return to our respective homerooms.

"Just staying home. Enjoy your trip, Leo." She smiled and walked through the doorway and down the hall.

My eyes watched her meander through other kids in the corridor. Just when I was ready to turn in the other direction toward my homeroom, Jessie turned back and looked at me. She locked eyes with me and smiled.

Our family made the three-hour trip to Ohio and arrived at my grandparents' house before noon on Thanksgiving. The house was filled with the wonderful aromas of pumpkin, turkey, and stuffing. We visit them only about four times a year, even though they're not that far away.

Brandon and I enjoy ourselves because our grandparents really dote on us, but Mom and Dad always seem a little tense and unnatural around them. Mom said she never had much in common with her parents and enjoys Grandma Lily's company more. She's only shared a few childhood stories with us, and she rarely even sees her sister who lives in Denver. Any time I've asked about visiting any of them, her answer is always that she's too busy and we're all the family she needs.

Grandma Peters never allows any of us in her kitchen while she prepares dinner. She had set up drinks, snacks, and dips for us in the family room, and our orders were to just relax until dinner. Some of our grandparents' friends joined us for the actual dinner, which was very formal.

My grandparents were gracious and kind when we visited, but we never shared any lively conversations or enjoyable moments. The stiffness and formalities created an environment that was very different from our celebrations at home.

We went to church on Saturday night with my grandparents, and my parents decided to leave for home early Sunday morning. My mom used the excuse that the weather looked bad for Monday, but I sensed that she and Dad just wanted to leave.

It was not even noon when we arrived home. Since we didn't eat anything on the road, Mom made us a big brunch. Already she seemed less tense and happier. It was strange the power that parents held over their children. I knew I was really blessed. We might not be a model family in every way, but I wouldn't trade what we had with anyone.

Chapter 20

The Christmas holiday season reached its peak shortly after Thanksgiving. Radio stations played nonstop carols, every commercial on TV showed a person or animal in a Santa hat, and my mom and Grandma Lily baked hundreds of cookies.

My family was busy every night either attending Brandon's hockey games and practices or taking trips to the mall to do Christmas shopping.

Anytime we went to the mall, my mom and dad headed off to do some shopping. They gave me and Brandon a lecture about safety and then designated a time and a place to meet them. They usually required only an hour, which was plenty of time for me.

Brandon would wander off to meet someone or occasionally spend time looking for things for himself. Brandon took after my mom. He loved buying clothes and had a special fondness for shoes. He would shop and take a picture of what he liked with his cell. Then he'd send it to my mom so she would know exactly what he wanted.

I didn't care much about clothes. My mom usually bought stuff for me, and I also wore Brandon's hand-me-downs. I was almost as tall as Brandon, but he was much more muscular. His pants and jeans were not my size, but I could wear his tee shirts. I actually preferred the old, worn look rather than brand new.

We did not usually shop on Fridays because Brandon had hockey practice in the early evening. But since there was only a week and a half till Christmas, no games were scheduled and most practices were canceled. So, even though the closets at home were already jammed with unwrapped presents, my mom wanted to make one last sweep of the stores for some bargains.

"This is the last time I want to shop," she said, almost with regret. "I've got to get all the gifts wrapped and put them under the tree. But, the circulars advertised some real bargains, and it won't hurt to look."

We split up at the food court, and everyone went their separate ways. I had no desire to go anywhere because the crowds were so thick. I walked over to Wendy's and got myself a large Frosty. There weren't many tables available, but I managed to find a small one tucked in the corner. There was only one chair, so that's probably why it was empty.

I played with the swirls in my Frosty and was doing a great job of making it last. I figured that, with any luck, I could make it last fifteen minutes. After that, I planned to waste some time in the bookstore. I used my spoon to make some designs in the ice cream, but it was starting to lose its thickness.

"Got any left for me, Leo?" Jessie's voice was coming from the plants and decorations that were on a wall beside me.

I heard a giggle, and then Jessie appeared around the corner. She had lots of shopping bags in her hands.

"I'd sit down with you, but it looks like that's not even an option." She rested the bags on my table.

I wiped some ice cream from my chin and tried to get out of my seat. "You can sit here. I'll look for another chair."

"Sit down, Leo. I'm only kidding. I've got to meet my parents in about five minutes. They dropped me off so I could finish my Christmas shopping, and they went to the grocery store. I have to wait for them outside by the mall entrance."

"Let me walk you there, Jessie. I can help you carry your bags. I'm done anyway." I tossed the half full container into the trash and reached for her bags.

"Thanks, Leo, I could use some help. Most of these bags are actually for me. I can always find things for myself when I'm trying to shop for others."

We made our way through the food court crowd and finally reached a more open area. We walked side by side for a while until we got to the doors of the mall entrance.

"They should be here soon if you'd like to go, Leo. I'm okay."

"I don't have to meet my parents for an hour, so I've got no place to go."

We placed her bags on a bench by the doorway. She looked out the window scanning the area for her parent's car. Then she turned and looked up at me.

She had that sadness in her eyes, a place where a few minutes ago there was a sparkle.

"Leo, . . ." she hesitated and then she started again, "Leo, I have so much to explain to you. I just really don't know where to begin."

These were words I had wanted to hear for months, but all I felt now was embarrassment. My head dropped as I looked down at my shoes. I knew my face was red, and my body was shaking. I braced myself, expecting her to give me an explanation for why she didn't care about me. I waited for the "but I still want to be your friend" line.

"Leo, I've really missed you. I wish I could explain everything to you, but . . . I don't really know yet if I can. But, Leo, it had nothing to do with you, really . . . nothing to do with us."

"You can tell me when you're ready, Jess." I slid my hands into my pants pockets to hide how much they were shaking. I still couldn't look her in the eyes.

"It was a personal issue, and even though I'm not ready to talk about it yet, I know that when I am . . . well, Leo, you're the one I'll want to talk to first."

"Jessie, please . . . just tell me. Was there someone else this past summer? Is there someone else now?"

"Leo, there's never been anyone but you." This time her eyes fell to the floor, and *her* face reddened.

She kept her eyes down for what seemed like minutes. The whole time, my heart was beating so hard that I could scarcely breathe. Finally she looked up, and I could see a few tears in the corners of her eyes.

"Oh, Leo," she sighed. She took a step closer to me and put her face at my chest. My hands came out of my pockets and wrapped around her. She started sobbing gently into my chest, and I held her tight. Then I dared to kiss the top of her head, and I reached down and wiped away some of her tears. She tilted her face up towards me and closed her eyes. We kissed. I stopped and looked into her eyes, and then we kissed again. All the sounds and people and things around us vanished for those few precious seconds.

Jessie giggled sweetly. "Leo, I never thought that I'd be kissing you at the mall." She wiped some of her remaining tears away.

I was still too mesmerized to say anything. My hand slid into hers, and we sat down beside her pile of shopping bags. My knees were still shaking, and it was a release to take the weight off them.

We sat and smiled at each other and said nothing.

"Oh!" Jessie said and stood up quickly and ran to the entrance window. "I forgot to look for our car!"

First she looked out the window, and then she actually stepped outside the door to be sure she could see everywhere. She shook her head.

"They're late, but I know they'll be here soon." She zipped up her jacket and pulled her hat and gloves from her pockets. "I'd better wait outside. I think the cold air will do me some good."

"Jessie—" I needed some assurance that this moment wouldn't be forgotten as soon as she walked out the door.

She read the look on my face. "I'll email you when I get home. Okay, Leo?"

I nodded in agreement, and then a horn beeped.

"That's them now." She grabbed her bags and walked to the doorway. She turned around slightly and smiled. Then she slipped out the door and into the winter air.

My parents, especially my mom, were in a shopping frenzy that night. When we all met in front of the bookstore, Dad's body was barely visible behind the bags he was trying to juggle. As soon as he saw me, he dropped the bags at my feet.

"Your turn, Leo. I've been a Sherpa long enough."

Brandon and a congregation of his friends were nearby, and he grinned and nodded in conversation. I was pretty sure the strawberry blonde beauty was his new girl of the month.

Mom checked her list and went through a collection of holiday coupons. "The mall is open till midnight tonight. So many things are on sale, it's hard to pass them up."

Dad looked as eager as I to get on the road. Brandon would probably like to stay, though. If I didn't play my cards right, we wouldn't get home till every store closed.

"I don't really feel so great, Mom," I said in a voice that sounded weak and sickly. "I'd really just like to go home and go to bed."

My dad chimed in quickly, "Joyce, if Leo doesn't feel well, we'd better head home. There'll be more bargains after the holidays."

Reluctantly, my mom agreed. Brandon talked my parents into allowing him to stay and catch a ride home with one of his friends' parents.

It took almost forty minutes for a typical twenty-minute drive home because of Christmas shopping traffic. I headed for my room as soon as we got home. I was still playing the "I'm sick" card, so my parents didn't question my quick disappearance. I sat at my desk and opened my email. My heart sank as I saw nothing but junk mail. Maybe Jessie was just playing me. I pictured her calling her friends and laughing as she recounted our kisses at the mall. Doubt crept into everything that had happened. I wondered if she could lie so convincingly and even fake tears.

I decided not to check my email for another half hour. If there was no email, I had been played.

The smell of popcorn drew me downstairs. My mom and dad were sitting at the kitchen island sharing a bag of microwaved popcorn and sipping some wine.

"Feeling better, Leo?" my mom asked as she threw a handful of popcorn in her mouth. "Maybe a snack will help."

I decided on a ginger ale and a bowl of chips and then headed to the family room. Every channel on television played Christmas specials, so I settled on watching part of one of my favorite movies of the season, *The Christmas Story*. Ralphie had just received a "D" on his essay and read the infamous words "You'll shoot your eye out," which his teacher had written across the page.

I felt a lot like Ralphie. We both had high expectations, but we both kept being let down.

I finished the bowl of chips and most of my soda. *The Christmas Story* lured me in, and before I realized it, an hour had passed. I said goodnight to my parents and made my way to my computer desk. Anxiety filled my body. My mind went into a protection mode—blank, foggy, out of body. Robotically I opened my email. There, on the screen, was an email from Jessie. I took a deep breath and opened the letter.

Leo,

Christmas magic is in the air
I felt its chill as you kissed my hair.
I felt its warmth with your sweet embrace
Enchanted by the smile on your face.
Spellbound, breathless, I felt it all
That Christmas magic at the mall!

Jessie

I lost track of how many times I read the words. The mere fact that she had composed a poem as our first written communication since June made all the planets in the universe align. My Jessie was back! Whatever personal troubles had plagued her, and still remained hidden in her heart, could not break the bond that we had.

Her email had been sent over twenty minutes ago. I needed to respond quickly so that she would know I felt the same magic that she had experienced.

Jessie,

Wonder and enchantment surrounded me too
But, it was not Christmas magic, it was only you
Who filled me with the warmth and chill.
Your spellbinding presence that is with me still.

Leo

A few minutes after I sent that poem, Jessie wrote back.

Leo,

I can't wait to see you again. Tomorrow won't work, but if possible, maybe Sunday? Goodnight. Think about me and send me an email tomorrow.

Jessie

Chapter 21

AN HOUR LATER I was still awake. I snuggled up to my pillow and smiled into the night air. My own private movie, *The Magic at the Mall*, played in my head over and over again. It was now my personal Christmas special, and I couldn't get enough of it. I didn't even want to sleep. My energy level was on par with the Energizer Bunny on caffeine. When the dial on my digital clock turned to a blinking two-zero-zero, I got up, wrapped myself in a blanket, and made my way to the family room. I was still smiling when I hit the remote.

This was the marathon weekend of *The Christmas Story*. Ralphie was tearing open his BB gun and was wearing the same smile I had. Yep, I thought . . . you and me, Ralphie, we are kindred souls. It was a long difficult road, but we both got what we wanted for Christmas!

I fell asleep on the couch and awoke to the smell of bacon. Dad had risen early and started cooking bacon and eggs for himself. It was only seven o'clock. Mom would be in bed for another hour, and Brandon would sleep till noon.

My dad looked a little startled when I joined him in the kitchen.

“Fell asleep on the couch last night. Hope I didn’t scare you.”

“Nah, it takes a lot more than a teenager with matted hair and morning breath to scare your old man. Want some?” Dad motioned towards the bacon omelet in the pan.

“I’ll have a little if you don’t mind sharing.”

Dad slid a portion of the omelet onto a plate for me. He grabbed his muffin from the toaster and put the rest of the egg on a plate for himself.

We sat at our kitchen island and finished eating in a few minutes. Dad smiled at me as he grabbed my empty plate. He tousled my hair with his free hand.

“Go back to bed, Leo—you definitely need more beauty sleep.”

When I got to my bedroom, I went directly to my computer desk. I shot off an email to Jessie to let her know that I was awake. I included my cell number, which she didn’t yet have, and told her she could call or email me when she was awake. The weather was damp and cold that weekend, so I suggested that we meet at the mall. I could probably have my parents drop me there sometime in the afternoon.

I hopped into the shower and was clean and dressed by eight thirty. I quickly cleaned my room and finished my only school assignment for that weekend. I still felt energized. Life was so good that I didn’t need or want sleep.

My cell phone rang at nine thirty. Jessie’s sweet voice whispered, “Morning, early bird. What got you out of bed so early? Don't you like sleeping in on Saturdays? It's so dark and dreary that I had a hard time getting out of bed at nine."

"The smell of bacon got me moving this morning. I'll probably need a nap this afternoon."

"My day won't be over until about seven tonight. I'm doing some volunteer work for a women's shelter downtown. You know—sorting donations and wrapping them as Christmas gifts."

"Wow," I said sincerely, "that's great."

"It has been great, Leo. The women at the shelter really struggle every day. It makes me realize how blessed I am."

We talked for a few more minutes trying to figure out when we could meet up on Sunday. But we each had too many family things going on that day, and no part of the day was free for both of us. Now Jessie had to leave because her mom was waiting to drive her to the donation site. We agreed to think about a plan for Sunday and talk later that night.

"Gotta go, Leo. Think about me."

I just mumbled a hasty goodbye. I didn't tell her that most of the hours of my day were spent thinking about her.

Jessie called my cell at nine o'clock that night. She sounded tired, but said she had a good day. She and her parents had gone out to dinner after they picked her up from her volunteer work, and she had arrived home only a few minutes ago. The only plan that seemed possible for Sunday was to meet on the corner around seven and take a walk for as long as we could stand the cold.

"Just wear lots of layers, Jessie," I said laughing, "because I'll want to stay out with you for as long as you can stand it!"

I was waiting outside her home a few minutes before seven. I told my parents that I needed to get some exercise and fresh air. My mom offered to come with me. She said that a walk would do her good. But I quickly talked her out of it by telling her I would be jogging, not just walking.

The neighborhood was completely dark except for the Christmas lights that adorned most houses. The sky was cloudy and the air cold and damp. I looked over at the Delaney house, which was decorated with soft white lights along the roof and entrance. A green flood light streamed onto three white wooden deer in the yard. Jessie had told me when we were together last Christmas that her dad made them himself. A few lights shown in the upstairs windows, and a light flickered from the fireplace that was visible through a large window downstairs. I pictured Jessie cozied up on her couch with a book in her hands and her face glowing from the light of the fire.

Before I could imagine myself beside her, a shadowy figure emerged from the back of the house. Jessie looked my way, and, as soon as I gave her a wave, she darted towards me. We were only inches apart when she stopped, looked me in the eyes, and smiled.

"Leo, I missed you so much." The words came out of her mouth with puffs of smoke from the winter's air. But my heart was pulsing warm blood through every part of my body. I barely let her finish the sentence. My lips were on her lips. It was a long, passionate kiss. It felt so good that it hurt.

When we finally stopped, we started laughing. There was so much joy in that moment that laughter was the only logical thing to do.

"Leo, I can't stay long. I snuck out the back door. My dad would never let me walk at night, even if he knew you were with me." She gave me a don't-be-mad-at-me look.

"Best five minute date I've ever had."

She punched me in the arm and kissed me quickly. "We'll have lots of five minutes together, Leo. Lots and lots."

After I watched her get safely back in the house, I took a jog around the neighborhood. My body was surging with that boundless energy again. I was running on Jessie power!

Chapter 22

WHEN JESSIE AND I SAW EACH OTHER on the bus Monday morning, we just waved. She sat down beside Katie just like always. After our five minute date on the corner, we talked for half an hour on our cells. We decided to ease into making our relationship public. With only seven days of school left before Christmas break, our secrecy would not be that difficult.

"Hey, Leo, see that?" Jordan poked my arm with his elbow. "Jessie just smiled at us! I must look particularly handsome this morning."

"Yep, that's right, Jordan," I said in a pseudo-serious tone. "You are a chick magnet, and I am not worthy to share a bus seat with you."

He turned to me and pretended to do a psychic stare into my eyes. "Something's up. My spidey sense is tingling. Want to tell me, or do I have to use my secret powers to find out?"

It really didn't take much urging for me to share a general description of my weekend. I left out most of the intimate details, but Jordan was now aware of my rejuvenated relationship with Jessie.

"Shut up!" he said when I finished the story. He sounded like some Valley Girl from the past.

"You've got to keep it quiet for a while, Jordan. Jessie and I just want to take it slow, at least till after Christmas."

"I'll keep it on the down low, bro. You can trust me, man."

Jordan might not have known what century he was in, or for that matter what gender he was, but I knew I could trust him.

The week went by so fast. Teachers were trying to cram in some last minute tests and assignments before our twelve-day Christmas break. But, at the same time, they were also trying to give us an opportunity to celebrate the season. We had some special assemblies, which included a presentation by the school choir and a particularly funny teacher talent show (or as we students like to refer to it, the teacher no-talent show). Even the cafeteria got into the spirit by renaming food on the menu. Snowman milk, Santa sausage, and reindeer waffles were on Friday's breakfast choices. It was the same bad food, just with different names.

Most of us had decorated our lockers for the season. I had one little snowflake dangling from the middle of my door. Jessie's locker was covered with cards and some silver tinsel. We made a point to talk to each other when we met in the hallways. Quite often we would stand in front of my locker. Jessie commented on the minimalist style of my decor.

"You need to spice it up a little, Leo," she said teasingly. "At least add a little tinsel."

When I approached my locker that Friday morning, Jessie had placed a little surprise on my locker door. A little stuffed angel teddy bear hung beside my snowflake. Jessie's school picture was pinned to the bear's face, and the bear's red tee shirt read "Hug me."

All that day, Jessie's girlfriends giggled or did a sing-songy "Hi, Leo!" when they saw me in the hall. Guys high-fived or punched me and said things like "Sweet" or "Hug me too, Leo."

Jessie had revealed our relationship, and her choice made me feel much more secure. Jessie would not have been so public if she weren't sure of how she felt. But, I admit, a part of me loved the secret aspect of our love. Our classmates would think we were just another school couple, and I knew we were so much more.

That weekend Jessie and I only managed to talk on our cells and send a few emails. She was doing volunteer work on Saturday, and I had lots of family things on Sunday. Jordan spent most of the day with me on Saturday. We played Xbox most of the afternoon, and then he stayed for dinner with my family.

For much of the day, Jordan was pumping me for information about my relationship with Jessie. I gave him as little information as possible. He was particularly concerned about our morning bus ritual.

"If you wanna sit with Jessie, it's okay with me," he said. "It wouldn't bother me at all to switch. That would give Katie a chance to enjoy my company."

"I think we'll keep things the same. You might be a little too much for Katie that early in the morning."

Monday and Tuesday were our only school days that coming week. Christmas fell on a Friday, and that meant almost two weeks of Christmas break. The atmosphere at school was pretty relaxed. Teachers knew we didn't have much attention span. In most classes we completed worksheets for review or did some assigned readings.

Jessie and I agreed not to make too many changes in our daily routine. The only big change at school was in Language Arts. We chose to move our seats to the middle of the classroom so that we sat beside each other. At lunch we still sat with our own friends.

Jessie brought up the subject of how we could hook up over the Christmas break. Neither of us wanted to say much about our relationship to our families.

Jessie thought that her dad would give her the "you're too young" speech, and I pictured my mom just saying things like, "Oh how cute. Leo has a girlfriend!" I knew for a fact that Brandon would tease me constantly.

So although our friends knew, our families were still in the dark.

Chapter 23

WE DEVISED A PLAN to have a secret Christmas. We would have our parents drop us off at the mall on the Monday after Christmas, under the pretense that we were hanging out with friends. It would be our first real date—a lunch at the food court and a movie at the mall cinema.

We hadn't spoken about a gift exchange, but I was already prepared. I had purchased a pair of earrings for Jessie in the summer when I was on my family vacation. Of course, I never gave them to her. Now the little butterfly earrings would be her Christmas gift.

My one regret with our private Christmas was that Jessie would not experience a Harrison family Christmas. Christmas Eve and Christmas Day were always some of the most memorable times for me. Even though our local family was small—just us and Grandma Lily—we had a great extended family and friends.

My mom's best friend since grade school, Karen Schilling, and her husband, Mark, and two daughters, Michelle and Nicole, always spend Christmas Eve with us. We'd have a grab-bag gift exchange, eat way too much food, and listen to childhood stories about the good old days.

The evening usually ended with a song fest. My dad and Mark both had great singing voices. They harmonized and did beautiful renditions of our favorite carols. The night ended with "Silent Night," and then the Schilling family would leave. Even though they lived only forty minutes from us, we usually only saw them a few other times during the year.

On Christmas morning, we'd open our presents and sip hot chocolate and eat Christmas cookies. Grandma Lily met us at morning Mass. We went home for a light lunch, and later enjoyed a huge holiday dinner. The dinner was followed by more childhood and family stories. Most of them focused on Christmas tales about me and Brandon or memories of my grandfather.

Grandpap John died before I turned two, so these stories were important to me. Grandma Lily had a talent for description, and I felt like I knew him well. It was apparent from the way everyone talked about him that he was just a good, regular guy who was loved very much. Sometimes my Grandma Lily would tear up a little during some of the stories, but mostly she laughed and smiled as she remembered her married life.

We were lucky to have her spend so much time with us. My Uncle Charlie and Uncle Ken and his family visited from the other side of Pennsylvania for a few days after Christmas. They stayed with my grandmother's house—the house where my uncles and dad had lived as children and where my grandparents had spent most of their married life. That bond with family and dear friends was one of the many things I cherished about Christmas.

Jessie told me last year when we first became close, that her parents didn't have any real family. She said that her dad lost his mother and father before he was twenty, and his younger brother died just a few years after that. As for Mrs. Delaney, she had endured a bad childhood and had left home when she was only eighteen. She had no relationship with any of her family after that.

So, Jessie had no grandparents or other relatives in her life. It felt so strange when I imagined the isolation of their lifestyle. Jessie said that they sometimes shared Christmas Eve with some neighborhood families, but Christmas Day was just Jessie and her parents.

The final school day before Christmas break was a half day. Jessie and I reluctantly parted at our corner after our bus ride home. I was home for only two hours when I wondered if I could make it through the next few days without seeing her. So, rather than endure the loneliness, I called Jessie on her cell to tell her that I already missed her. During the course of our conversation, I expressed my concern over her facing what I considered a lonely Christmas. I made a remark about how great the Harrison holiday festivities would be.

"My Grandma Lily makes the best sausage stuffing, and my mom's turkey gravy makes anything taste good!

I wish you could come over to enjoy some really great home cooking, Jessie."

It wasn't a comment to slam her mom's cooking. Jessie herself had often made remarks about many of their bad meals.

"All three of us do some cooking on Christmas, Leo. It may not be as great as your dinner, but you don't have to pity me. My family might not be the same as yours, but that doesn't mean we don't enjoy our time together too! Not everyone's family can be as perfect as yours!"

Jessie did not even try to hide her anger. I knew I had crossed a line, but I honestly did not mean to hurt her or belittle her family.

"I didn't mean it that way, Jess." I was really floored by her tone. "I guess it's just hard for me to imagine your family dynamics."

"Leo, I don't think you could ever imagine my family dynamics!" She hung up the phone.

I waited a few minutes and redialed, but it went right to voice mail. My heart beat rapidly as I worried about how to word my apology. I honestly didn't understand why she had become so upset.

After five attempts to call her back, which all resulted in voice mail responses, I decided to send her an email.

Jessie,

I'm sorry. Please don't be angry with me. As usual, the words came out wrong. I didn't mean to insult your family. What I meant to say was that I just wish the two of us could share Christmas together.

Leo

I left almost the same message on her cell. At midnight I still had not heard back from her. Was this going to be a replay of summer? I was still in the dark about that. Now, because of my insensitive remarks, I might have lost her for good.

It was a restless night for me. Several times I checked my cell and emails. I even imagined sneaking over to her house and throwing stones at her window until she would answer me. My fear of Mr. Delaney was the only thing stopping me.

When I awoke around ten, I felt the old sickening feeling that had been gone for weeks. I wanted so badly for that stupid phone call never to have happened. I grabbed my cell from my nightstand. No missed calls or messages. I called Jessie. No answer.

The rest of the day was filled with jobs from my mom and dad. I wrapped some presents, cleaned my room, and helped my mom get the house ready for the holiday. Dad came home from work a little early, so we ate before six.

Since I still hadn't heard from Jessie, I told my parents I was going to take a little after-dinner jog. I was on "our corner" by seven. It was dark outside and cold enough to make my ungloved hands go numb. I could see the Delaney house, and, except for the outside Christmas lights, it was totally dark. Mrs. Delaney's car was not in the driveway.

I ran for about fifteen minutes. Long enough for my body to start sweating. I made one last pass of the Delaney house, and then headed home.

It was one o'clock on Thursday, Christmas Eve, before I heard from Jessie.

Leo,

I know that sometimes I make my family sound strange and dysfunctional, but they are my family. I know you weren't trying to be mean, but your comments did hurt me. There is so much you don't know about my parents, and now I wonder if I can ever share some of those things with you.

Every family is different. The perfect family only exists in fairy tales.

Jessie

Her email sounded hurt, not angry. It just made me sicker to think that I could have hurt her so much with those stupid comments.

Jessie,

I know how much you love your family. Truthfully, I have always envied the relationship you have with your dad. When you tell me about working on projects with him and how you two talk during your lunches together, it makes me feel like I'm missing something with my own dad.

I'm so sorry that my words about your family were so hurtful. Please forgive me.

Leo

My cell played "Jingle Bells" a few minutes later. It was a special ring I had assigned for Jessie.

"Leo, thanks for the words about my dad. I'm still hurt, but I'm not as mad as I was. It's just . . . well, I'm pretty sensitive about them."

"Jessie, you were right to be angry. That's the way I would feel if someone said something about my family, too. I'm such an idiot."

"Let's both agree to that and move on," she said with a gentle laugh. "I just want to wish you a merry Christmas Eve before you start all your celebrating."

"It would be merrier if I could be with you. Will you call me tomorrow? Maybe between two and four would be good."

"I'll call. I've got to wish you a Merry Christmas, don't I?"

"Jessie, we're still on for our date, right?"

"Already have my ride lined up, and the movie picked out."

"Merry Christmas Eve, Jessie."

That phone call was the best Christmas gift she could have given me. I made a personal pledge to think before I made any comments about family or friends. Jessie was important to me. I needed to be more sensitive to her feelings.

After our Christmas Eve celebration with the Schillings, the quiet Christmas morning with my family was relaxing. I often found my thoughts shifting to Jessie. I was aching to share holiday moments with her. During Mass that morning, all the singing from the choir and the beautiful decorations in our church just made her absence more difficult.

My whole family was exhausted by one o'clock Christmas Day. We had partied past midnight with the Schillings the night before and then opened presents around seven in the morning. Church was extra long, and when we returned home, most of us had barely enough energy to eat a light lunch.

The turkey was already in the oven, and Grandma Lily had everything else under control. So, while we waited for dinner, everyone took time to rest. My mom and dad went to the couch to watch TV, and Brandon and I made a beeline to our rooms.

I had my cell in my pocket and hoped Jessie would call soon. Out of habit, I checked my email. Jessie had sent an email around ten this morning. Usually we would have been home at that time, but Christmas Mass is so crowded that we left early to get a parking place.

Leo,

Someday we'll share a Christmas, with friends and family too.
We'll make some beautiful memories, the way our parents do.
So that when we are together, old and very gray,
We'll look to one another, and one of us will say,
"Remember, my sweet darling, the way things used to be
As we opened all our presents under the Christmas tree?"
We'll cuddle by the fire and smile as we reminisce
About a Christmas morning when we shared a Christmas kiss.

Jessie

The poem was a wonderful Christmas morning gift from Jessie. It made me imagine the two of us as a family, and it made me think that Jessie saw a real future for our relationship. Did I dare to tell her that, not only did I imagine a long future with her too, but I could not imagine a future without her?

In the middle of attempting to put all those feelings down, I heard the "Jingle Bells" ring of my cell.

"Merry Christmas, and a ho-ho-ho," I said in my best Santa voice. "Did you get everything you wanted for Christmas?"

Her sweet laugh filled my ear. "Merry Christmas to you too. And, yes, I got everything and more. What about you? Was Santa good to you too?"

"Why wouldn't he be? He knew I was a good boy. Of course, my favorite gift wasn't from Santa. It was a poem. I just read it a few minutes ago, Jess. I was trying to write you an answer, but I'm starting to feel the holiday blahs overcoming me. You know, that awful feeling after being up late and eating too much junk."

"Yeah, that's gonna hit me soon. I just had three cookies and a glass of hot chocolate for lunch."

Our conversation lasted quite long. Jessie listed the things she got for Christmas, and I told her a little about our visit from the Schillings. I tried not to sound too excited because I was afraid she might take it wrong.

In the background I heard her mom call her.

"Gotta go, Leo. We're having ham, and mom and I are going to try a recipe for cheesy scalloped potatoes that I found on the internet."

"Can I call you tonight? Maybe around ten?"

"It's a date. Talk to you then. Enjoy your Christmas feast."

"Jessie, . . . your poem . . . it really was the best gift."

"Tell me in person, Leo. Monday, our secret Christmas."

I decided to not even try and compose a poem back to Jessie. I went to my bed and covered myself with a Steeler throw blanket. My daydreams took me to Jessie's poem. I imagined us sitting on a couch in front of a Christmas fire and sharing a kiss.

Chapter 24

THE DAY AFTER CHRISTMAS my Uncle Charlie and Uncle Ken and his family came into town. They stayed with Grandma Lily, and everyone came to our house for a second Christmas celebration and another big family meal.

We hadn't seen them since our summer vacation, so there was a lot of catching up to do in a small amount of time. Our reunion lasted only a few days, and they were on the road early Sunday afternoon. Uncle Charlie headed home to Richmond, and Uncle Ken, Aunt Bev, Michael, and Julie went east to their home in Philadelphia.

Our house was quiet after that. It made me wonder again what Jessie and her parents did to occupy their vacation time, but I felt it would be dangerous to ask. Jessie's mom was on vacation from work, but I knew Mr. Delaney was keeping a regular work schedule.

I called Jessie's cell. She answered quickly, and I could hear a lot of voices in the background.

"Sorry, Jessie," I said. "Is this a bad time?"

"I can talk for a few minutes, Leo, but then I have to go help my mom. We're having a Christmas lunch and party for some of the ladies from the women's shelter. We have four moms here and five toddlers, so I can't talk long."

"You never cease to amaze me, Jessie." I hoped I sounded as sincere as I felt. My previous words and worries about the Delaney's having a boring holiday were sounding more and more stupid. They seemed to be having a holiday that was really in the spirit of Christmas.

"Mom and I baked and cooked all morning, and everyone just arrived a little while ago. We were just going to sit down and eat."

"When can I call you back, Jessie?"

"I'll call *you*, Leo. I don't know when we'll be done. Mom and I bought everyone some gifts too, so it might take a while."

After our call, I felt like such a jerk. I guess Jessie had been right to get angry with me. My sentiments about her Christmas were pitying and insensitive. It was arrogant for me to have a "my family's better than your family" attitude. Jessie and the whole Delaney family were full of surprises.

Jessie sent me a text later that day. It said she would call around eleven if that wasn't too late. I sent back a quick "ok."

When she called me a little before eleven, her voice was bubbly and excited. She shared some of the events of her Christmas lunch. The women were single moms. Many of them had left abusive relationships and were now struggling to support themselves and their children. The lunch was one of Jessie's favorite experiences ever.

"Leo, you can't believe how happy and grateful the moms were. Most of them were crying when they opened some of the little presents we had for them. They said it was the nicest Christmas they ever had! They just kept thanking us over and over again."

"Did they stay long?"

"The shelter's van came at five o'clock to pick them up. I wish they could have stayed so much longer. The little kids were so much fun to have around too. It was so great, Leo. Mom and I want to do something with them again soon. Maybe even do a monthly little gathering."

"Hey, Jess, I just happened to think. Maybe we could do a student council activity for them. At our last meeting we were brainstorming some things we could do as a service project for the community."

"Oh, Leo, that's a great idea. Let's talk about that on our date tomorrow."

The malls were as packed that Monday after Christmas as they were the week before the holiday. Everyone was exchanging gifts or looking for bargains. But, as crowded as everything was, it did not take me long to spot Jessie. She was scanning the movie banners along the walls in front of the theater. Her long brown hair rested on the shoulders of her tan ski jacket. Around her neck was a soft, teal-colored scarf that matched the gloves sticking from her jacket pockets. The closer I got to her, the more her beautiful green eyes shimmered.

"Merry Christmas, Leo," she said as she reached out to give me a hug. The hug was a little stiff and awkward, and we both laughed at our clumsy attempt to be relaxed and cool. She reached down and grabbed my hand. "Let's get inside—I've got the movie picked out already. It doesn't start for twenty minutes, but we can sit down and talk in there."

Jessie had chosen a romantic comedy, and since we were rather early, we had our choice of seats. She headed for a row almost exactly in the middle of the stadium seating. We removed our jackets and clumped them in an empty seat. When we finally settled into our seats, Jessie reached for my hand and leaned her head onto my shoulder. The fragrance of her hair was a mixture of coconut-scented shampoo and the crisp winter air. We sat for several minutes and just enjoyed the serenity of the moment.

Mustering up some courage, I kissed her hair and reached into my pocket. I slipped a red box with a white bow into Jessie's hand. "Merry Christmas," I whispered into her hair.

She unwrapped the package as carefully as I had wrapped it. Her smile and her eyes widened when she saw the butterfly earrings that were almost a perfect match to the necklace I had given her a year ago.

"Oh, Leo, what a perfect gift."

As validation of how perfect my gift was, she reached down and stroked the butterfly necklace that she was wearing.

"This necklace always makes me feel like you're with me. Now I'll have earrings that will give me a double dose of Leo." She gave me a cheek kiss that slid right into a lip kiss.

She looked at the gift box in her hand and smiled as she replaced the lid. "I'll put these on later. I don't want to chance dropping them and losing them on the floor of the theater."

She reached over to the seat beside her and slipped her hand into her purse. When she turned back to me, she was holding a rectangular box.

"I hope you like my gift for you, Leo. It's something that I made, so be careful what you say about it."

"I know I'll like it, Jessie," I said as I unwrapped the box.

The box held a wooden picture frame. Jessie's dad had made the frame, and she used a wood etching electric pen to burn the design into the wood. She had etched our names beautifully four times, once on each side of the frame. On each side she had used a different style and a different size for the letters. In between our names were hearts and butterflies. The frame surrounded a beautiful picture of Jessie—her school photo from October. Jessie was wearing a teal V-neck top. Around her neck was the butterfly pendant.

In the brief time it took to scan the frame and the picture, my mind assessed the time period. October was still a time when Jessie had distanced herself from me. The necklace made me realize that she still felt something for me then. I wanted so badly to ask her why she had been so engulfed in sadness and why she had alienated me all those months. But, this was not the time. I needed to express how touched I was with her gift.

"Jessie, I really don't know what to say. I would have loved any picture of you, but the frame makes it so special. I can't believe that you did the etching yourself! You always manage to surprise me with your talents."

She beamed with pride, and I sensed her joy in my reaction. I took her hands to my lips and kissed them.

"We need to replace the picture though, Leo. It should be a photo of the two of us."

The theater slowly filled, and the lights dimmed as some previews started. She put the frame back in her purse for safe storage, and then she placed her head on my shoulder. We held hands and watched the movie.

First date, perfect date,
Secret Christmas that was ours.
Hands entwined, knees aligned
Hearts swimming with desires.
A movie playing, some voices saying
Silly lines that made us laugh.
Gifts shared, heads paired,
Memories that will always last.

Chapter 25

OUR RELATIONSHIP CONTINUED to grow after we returned to school in January. We were considered a couple by all our classmates, and we were teased often. Following the celebrity trend of combining couples names, friends referred to us as "Jello."

Jessie and I took it all in stride. What others thought didn't really matter much. The written words of our emails kept our bond unique and private. Neither of us cared much for PDA, and we avoided the pattern of so many other school couples who abandoned friends and activities for each other. Our individual identities remained intact, and that made our moments alone together special.

At the beginning of February, posters announcing the upcoming school Valentine Dance appeared on the hallway bulletin boards. The dance was always a big event, especially for the girls.

I sent Jessie an email as soon as the date was officially announced at school.

My Fair Lady Jessie,

Wouldst thou do me the great honor of accompanying me to the Valentine Ball? Alas, thy sweet countenance shall be the inspiration that will give me the bravery to venture onto the field of battle (the dance floor).

Wouldst thou, couldst thou, be my valentine?

Sincerely yours,
Sir Leo the Lionhearted

I knew Jessie couldn't resist the romantic nature of my invitation. An email was actually easier for me than a spoken invitation anyway. I still found it difficult to express myself when I was face-to-face with her. My quiet nature and the fact that Jessie's presence still overwhelmed me added to my awkwardness.

Jessie's reply arrived within the hour of my invitation.

Sir Leo the Lionhearted,

Thy brave offer to enter the field of battle for me is one that I shall truly cherish for all the ages. How can I deny thee the opportunity to display thy valor and chivalry for all the realm to witness?

So, with great trust in your abilities, I accept thy invitation.

Your valentine,
Lady Jessie

As soon as I told my mother that I was going to the dance with Jessie, she could not control her insanity. She jumped in and volunteered to drive us and babbled about what I should wear. She was excited and, of course, curious about my relationship with Jessie. She was genuinely surprised that I had any girlfriend and was particularly happy that it was Jessie.

"You are very lucky to have her as a girlfriend, Leo. She is so adorable, and she always impressed me with her respectful attitude."

I just nodded in agreement. The inevitable barrage of questions was coming. My mom needed details about our friendship and about the dance. She didn't disappoint and felt no embarrassment over asking me if we were in a "romantic" relationship.

My intent was to tell her as little as possible, but I found myself sharing things easily. My mother's enthusiasm and joy was contagious. It was nice to be able to talk to her about Jessie, and I knew she would tell Brandon, my dad, and Grandma Lily, too.

"So, Leo, you need to find out what color dress Jessie is wearing. I'll order a corsage and find you a tie that complements what she wears. Oh, I'll have to check to see if you have a suit that fits."

"Most of the guys don't even wear suits, Mom. All I really need is a dress shirt and a tie. But I'll find out from Jessie about her dress color. Thanks for offering to get the corsage. I don't think I'd know what to order."

A dusting of snow covered the roads on the Friday night of the Valentine Dance, but the temperatures were going to stay in the thirties. Mom had found a nice gray sports jacket of Brandon's that fit me, and she bought me black dress pants and a white shirt. My tie was gray, black, and red striped. According to Mom, I couldn't look cuter.

We agreed that she and Dad could take some pictures of me at home. I gave strict orders to Mom not to ask to take pictures of me and Jessie when we picked her up. A professional photographer was scheduled to be at the dance. I had money and promised to order a package of pictures. I was nervous about everything, but I had the most concern about coming face-to-face with Mr. Delaney.

Mom pulled carefully onto the Delaney's driveway. The lights were on outside, and snowflakes sparkled as they fell gently on the walkway. I walked slowly as my hands clutched the wrist corsage in its plastic container. Mrs. Delaney stepped out onto the porch before I made it to the door.

"Leo, you look so handsome!" she said. Her voice had a nervous quiver of excitement. She motioned to my mom to get out of the car.

"Come on, Joyce, we want to take some pictures before Leo and Jessie jump in the car. Come in and stay warm."

My mom did not need a second invitation. She jumped from the car with her cell in her hand.

In the Delaney's living room, we all assembled near the fireplace. Mr. and Mrs. Delaney greeted me and my mother and said that Jessie would be down shortly. Mrs. Delaney and my mom prepared for the photo op, and Mr. Delaney and I just stared awkwardly around the room.

I heard the gentle clearing of a throat, and we all turned toward a doorway into the living room. Jessie was posed, waiting for everyone's attention and approval.

Her long brown hair was braided to one side, and beautiful silver earrings accented her shimmering necklace. Her deep-red dress was strapless, and she wore black heels with open toes. Her eyes were accented with a touch of makeup, and her lips shimmered with red gloss. She could have easily passed for a college student.

We all whistled and wowed at her appearance, and soon we both endured the flashes from cameras and cells as we posed for pictures. Whenever possible, I would sneak a look at Mr. Delaney. His face showed nothing but pride and love for Jessie, but he was fidgety and nervous. Jessie was right—an only child had a lot of parental pressure.

The school gymnasium was packed for the dance. My classmates were barely recognizable in their dressy attire. But there was no doubt in my mind that Jessie was the most beautiful girl there.

Music blasted, and chatter and laughter filled the gymnasium. My shyness about dancing kept me off to the side during fast songs. Jessie went out with the crowd, and I just smiled at her obvious joy in dancing and celebrating.

But, we danced together to all the slow songs. The shimmering lights, the romantic music, and the feeling of having Jessie in my arms was hypnotic. When the DJ announced the last song, I could barely believe the night was over. Our bodies swayed rhythmically to the music, and I held Jessie close.

I bent down and whispered into her ear. "I love you, Jessie Delaney. More than I ever thought was possible."

"Oh, Leo," she sighed, "I love you too. I love you, Leo Harrison. More than anyone or anything."

A few weeks later, the professional pictures from the Valentine Dance arrived in the mail. My mom opened them before I even saw the envelope. Except for a strange twist of my lip as I smiled, I looked rather dashing. Jessie, of course, looked perfect.

My mom cut up the sheets of photographs and positioned all the pictures on our kitchen island. She designated one each of the wallet sizes for her, Dad, and Grandma Lily. She was kind enough to allow me to have three. One of the 5x7s joined a framed collection of family photos that included a picture of Brandon at his first formal dance. I took the rest of the pictures to my room.

After removing Jessie's school picture, I placed our valentine photo in the frame. I didn't mark any date or information on the back of the photo. The memory of the day Jessie and I first spoke the words "I love you" was etched into my heart, just as deeply as our names were etched into the picture frame.

Chapter 26

OUR FAMILY TOOK A SHORT TRIP to visit my Uncle Ken and his family in Philadelphia for Easter break in early April. It was the first long-term separation Jessie and I had in the five months we were together.

We talked every day on our cell phones while I was away. But fear still lingered in me about an extended time away from Jessie. She still had not explained the mysterious change in her personality that developed over last summer. Occasionally her eyes would gloss over with a haunted, distant look. Her mood became serious, and she seemed far away. But it was nothing that lasted or impacted our relationship. Though I was curious, I was not inclined to question her about it. Leave well enough alone—that was my motto.

Our status as a couple became a natural part of my family life. Brandon no longer teased me about Jessie, and my mother quit acting giddy and excited when Jessie was around. Jessie came to our house occasionally after school, but she usually only stayed a short while.

Mom thought it would be nice if Jessie met Grandma Lily and had a nice dinner with the whole family. It was the last Sunday in April, and the bright yellow daffodils had popped out of the ground. Trees tentatively started to blossom, and lawns turned lush and green. The neighborhood bustled with joggers, bikers, and walkers.

Grandma Lily was excited about meeting Jessie and prepared for our big Sunday dinner days in advance. The menu choice was a big concern. She pelted me with questions as she leafed through some cookbooks in our kitchen.

"What's Jessie's favorite dinner, Leo? Does she eat salad? Maybe you could pick two good desserts for me to make. How about my famous chocolate layer cake and some snickerdoodles? Everyone likes chocolate or cinnamon."

I was somewhat nervous about the dinner. It was the first time Jessie would meet not only Gram, but Brandon too. I had already asked Mom to make sure that Brandon would not say or do anything that would embarrass me. But, anyone who has siblings knows that they can't be totally trusted not to try to make you look stupid.

Jessie was excited about the dinner and did not seem intimidated at all. She decided she would like to attend Sunday Mass with us too.

The whole Harrison family piled into our van at ten-forty that Sunday morning. As soon as we pulled into the Delaney driveway, Jessie stepped out onto the porch. She wore a pale yellow jacket over a gray and yellow floral dress. Her hair was pulled back, and soft little curled strands framed her beautiful face.

Brandon gave a whistle from his seat. "Wow, Leo, you are one lucky dude. You might just get some brotherly competition over this girl!"

Mom quickly glared at him. Words from her were not always necessary.

By the time we arrived at church, Jessie seemed totally comfortable with everyone. My family was on their good behavior and knew they had most of the day to get to know her. Even my mom controlled her natural urge for nervous chatter.

We filled a whole pew in the middle of our church. Jessie squeezed between me and Grandma Lily. As we waited for Mass to start, Gram answered some questions that Jessie posed, and she pointed out some of the statues and traditional parts of the church.

When Mass was over Jessie was full of more questions and comments. "You do so much up and down stuff and kneeling. It's a good thing I had some breakfast this morning."

Grandma Lily laughed. "You have to keep people awake, Jessie. But, Catholics do love their rituals. I always found it comforting. No matter where you go or what language the Mass is in, you can follow everything."

"It was beautiful. Your choir was wonderful. I'm amazed at the difference in the style of music. Yours has a more mystical and reverent sound than the music at our church. I don't know which I enjoy more."

Mom and Dad went off to say hello to some friends, and Gram suggested that I give Jessie a brief church tour. I showed her the Stations of the Cross around the sides of the church and explained a little about the life of St. Anthony, whose statue was in a little alcove on the side.

When we approached the statue of the Blessed Mother at the front left of the church, Jessie got that pensive, sad look in her eyes. She asked some questions about the Rosary, and then she knelt on a kneeler at the base of the statue.

I knelt beside her and watched as her eyes scanned the statue from top to bottom. Her eyes went back to the top, and she seemed to stare directly into Mary's eyes.

"Recite the Hail Mary for me, Leo. I've heard it before, but I don't know all the words."

So with Jessie beside me staring into the eyes of the Blessed Mother, I began the words I had known since first grade: "Hail Mary, full of grace . . ."

The prayer ended and Jessie smiled. She was still looking up at Mary's face.

"You know, Leo," she said, as she finally looked at me, "there is something very comforting about knowing that a loving mother will be there to greet us when we die."

She stood up and grabbed my hand. The solemn moment disappeared as quickly as it came. We walked together to the back of church and found my family.

That moment at the statue of the Blessed Mother felt rather odd, but I didn't give it much more thought that day. But a few days later, Jessie emailed me a poem she wrote.

The Eyes of a Child
Oh mother in heaven, looking down on me,
In my small life, what do you see?
Am I the daughter who makes you proud?
Or am I just a face, lost in a crowd?
Reach down to me and lift me high
Into your arms I wish to fly
In your embrace I'll find sweet rest
That only comes at a mother's breast.

We dropped Jessie at home after church that Sunday. She wanted to change into more comfortable clothes and would just walk to our house when she was ready. Shortly after one, she arrived at our home and was welcomed by the smell of our early dinner.

Her visit was so special that we used our dining room. Mom pulled out her best dishes; fresh flowers and floral napkins adorned the table. Dips, crackers, and fruit kept us satisfied until our meal was ready at three. The conversation flowed so naturally that I wondered why I ever worried.

Jessie was charmed and fascinated by my grandmother. She sat at our kitchen island and watched Gram move around the kitchen. She listened as Gram told her about how she learned to cook only shortly after she and my grandfather were married.

We spent a wonderful afternoon eating and talking. Jessie was relaxed and casual as she engaged in conversation with everyone in the family. Brandon even managed to hold back his natural tendency to talk mostly about himself, and he charmed Jessie with stories about me as a little boy.

Brandon had a six o'clock hockey practice, and he and Dad began getting ready around five. I said that I would walk Jessie home, so Gram wrapped up some cake and cookies for Jessie to give to her parents.

"Leo is so blessed to have such a wonderful girlfriend like you, Jessie," Gram said as she handed Jessie the plate of desserts. "I hope we see more of you." She gave Jessie a little sideways hug.

"I hope so too. Thank you so much for the wonderful afternoon. Maybe next time, I'll bring a dessert."

Jessie said some more goodbyes and thanked Mom and Dad. We walked out into the somewhat crisp evening air and headed toward Jessie's home.

"You are so lucky to have such a wonderful family, Leo. Especially to have your grandmother. Do you realize that's the first time I've had an extended conversation with anyone over the age of sixty-five?"

"Unless, of course, you count old Mrs. Trendle who taught us in seventh grade," I said as Jessie giggled. I still worried about bragging too much about my family, but I took the opportunity to bring up Jessie's family tree.

"Did you ever know any of your grandparents or aunts and uncles, Jessie?"

"My family history is pretty complicated, Leo," she said. Her eyes got that distant look again. "We'd need a whole day for me to explain it all. Anyway, let's just enjoy the walk home and have a few more of these snickerdoodles."

Jessie joined us every few weeks for Sunday Mass and our traditional early dinner. She spent time in the kitchen with Mom and Grandma Lily. The three of them liked to try new recipes, and Jessie said she enjoyed cooking so much that she considered becoming a chef.

She used some of her new skills in her volunteer work. She and her mom did some baking for the women's shelter and hosted a little springtime gathering at the Delaney home. Jessie decorated special cookies for the children and made treat bags for them often.

The women's shelter was one of Jessie's strong passions. She was pleased with me when I initiated a fundraising event with the help of our student council in early March. Our student council also decided to hold a bake sale in May. The money raised was used for Mother's Day gifts to the women at the shelter.

Our last days of the eighth grade school year remain some of my favorite memories. All of my classmates were aware that I was off to North Central in the fall.

Most of them would continue ninth grade in our middle school building.

Teachers and friends stopped me in the hall to wish me luck or say they would miss me. Even the janitor, Mr. Avery, patted me on the back and expressed a farewell.

During the last few weeks of that school year, some of my classmates displayed their creativity with postings on my locker. Cards, silly cartoons, and posters were taped to my locker door. Many of the drawings depicted a dragon (North Central's mascot) being slain, eaten, or crushed by a gladiator (our middle school mascot). One of my favorites was a wanted poster, complete with a rather good caricature of me, that read: Leo Harrison—Wanted for Treason. Reward: Two Cents.

Jessie laughed with me over the teasing, but she never missed an opportunity to make me feel guilty about my change of schools.

"Leo, couldn't you just stay until the end of ninth grade? Think of all the tuition money your parents would save." She used her sweet, baby voice and pouted her lips as she spoke.

I gave her the same response my father gave me on the subject. "Harrison tradition—it wouldn't be *tradition* without four years at North Central."

My conviction was not as strong as I let on. I worried about a new school and new friends, and I didn't like the idea of being separated from Jessie. I tried to sound confident and self-assured, probably because I needed to believe it would be okay.

"At least you won't have to worry about other girls at North Central, Jessie. I'll be sitting with hundreds of guys every day. The only females I'll see will be a few really old teachers. I'll probably spend most of my time imagining you surrounded by handsome ninth grade boys!"

On a cool Friday evening in the beginning of June, Jessie and I sat together on top of a picnic table at the park. The sky was pink, and the air smelled of blossoms and grass. In another hour the painted sky would grow dark, and we would need to head home. We had three days of school the next week, and three months of summer vacation ahead.

We spent so much time talking about the changes anticipated for the fall, but we never mentioned plans for the summer. My throat tightened with anxiety at any attempt to bring up summer plans, and my typical cowardly nature waited for Jessie to discuss that topic.

Her voice was noticeably nervous as she brought up the subject that evening. "Leo, I've decided not to go away to summer camp this year." She squeezed my hand reassuringly as she spoke. "I didn't have such a great time last year. Guess I'm just not the outdoorsy, camping type of girl."

This was a great opportunity for me to delve into the mystery of that summer, but I avoided asking a direct question. I looked up at the sky and alluded to our promise from last summer.

"Jessie, when we were apart last summer, I looked up at the sky almost every night at ten and tried to imagine what you were doing."

She looked up at the sky and then down at the ground. I waited nervously in the silence.

"I thought of you too," she began after several minutes. "But, I want to be honest with you. I didn't keep that promise. I was dealing with some confusing things in my life, and I had a hard time thinking about anything clearly."

"You can tell me or not tell me about what happened, Jessie. It's your decision."

She squeezed my hand, and her thumb gently massaged my knuckles. After staring blankly at the horizon for a few minutes, she spoke softly into the night air.

"What happened last summer is complicated. I haven't told you anything for a lot of reasons. There are things I'm still trying to sort out in my head. I'm not trying to be dramatic or secretive. I'm just not ready to tell anyone, not even you, Leo."

She turned and looked at me. No sadness was in her eyes or her voice when she said, "I don't ever want you to worry or doubt that I love you." She kissed me and snuggled closely to my side.

"Okay, Jess," I said with resignation. Although I longed for more information, her assurance of love satisfied me in that moment. She sounded more confused than troubled, and I was content just to be with her.

The annual Harrison reunion to Rehoboth Beach was shortened to two weeks that summer. My mother had a school seminar the last weeks of July, my cousin Michael enrolled in a basketball camp, and Brandon made some baseball tournament commitments. The complications of life gave me bonus time with Jessie. I was thankful then, and even more thankful now, for those extra few weeks.

An extra hour, an extra day,
To hold your hand, to hear you say,
I love you.

We had wonderful times together that summer. Sometimes we had a little spat over careless words or misunderstood intentions, but our joy in each other's company had no comparison. She was my best friend and my true love.

The images of our last times together are catalogued in my mind. Jessie spent time with me and my family at two Pirates games, a trip to the zoo, and many weekend dinners and cookouts. We swam and sunned at the pool, went to a few parties, and played laser tag with our friends. And, of course those private moments together when we took walks, held hands, and shared our deepest thoughts. I pull out a folder of memories whenever I am overcome with loneliness. Each time, I wonder if it eases my pain or makes it worse.

Chapter 27

MY FRESHMAN YEAR at North Central turned out to be a series of highs and lows. If I kept myself on cruise control and concentrated on my schoolwork and extracurriculars, everything was good. But now with November approaching, my golf activities were over, and I had too much down time.

Down time, of course, meant time to think about Jessie. Even though I had so many good memories about times we shared, images of Jessie in her coffin or lying lifeless at the accident scene managed to steal their way into my mind. I could only distract myself for a few hours with video games or homework, and I found it difficult to be with old friends who reminded me of times with Jessie.

Jordan called me every few weeks to catch me up on things at my old middle school. "Hey, bro, what's been happenin'?" was how he started every call. He was thoroughly enjoying his status as a ninth grader, the oldest class in that building. He said he was "dating" a really hot eighth grade girl. Of course, dating to Jordan could mean anything from sitting with her at lunch to hanging out with her and her other friends.

Jordan often asked me to go to some of the school basketball games with him and our old gang, but I always gave him an excuse about having too much homework. He knew my excuses were lame, but he never gave up on me. That's how I knew he was such a good friend. Anyone else would have stopped calling.

Friendship is a treasure
Not always such a pleasure
For, when the times get bad,
When someone you love is sad,
It's the loyalty you need to measure.

—Jessie Delaney, 8th grade

Jordan called me at the end of October. The annual middle school Halloween party was coming up, and he wanted to share his "awesome" idea for a Halloween costume. He was going to dress up as Einstein. He had already purchased a gray wig and fake mustache, and he came pre-equipped with the nerdy glasses. Just in case his peers wouldn't catch the resemblance, he had written $E=mc^2$ in white chalk on the back of a rumpled, old, black sports jacket that belonged to his dad.

"Chicks go for smart, older men, Leo. So I've got my bases covered . . . ain't nobody smarter and older lookin' than Einstein."

I wished him luck and gave him the courtesy of not asking what happened to his eighth grade girlfriend.

"Let me know how your plan works, Jordan. Take some good selfies and send them to me too."

Most Catholic schools aren't keen on celebrating Halloween. Some elementary schools allow small parties where students can dress in costumes, but it is usually frowned upon as an irreligious holiday.

North Central men certainly wouldn't celebrate, but it's hard for some teachers to let holidays pass without any activity. So, Mrs. Brunline, the other Language Arts teachers, and the art and drama department teachers decided to plan a three-day academic unit on the master of creepiness, Edgar Allan Poe. They had blocked off three afternoons when we would explore some of Poe's work, choose one of them, and prepare and practice a presentation.

The teachers split us into groups of about fifteen, each composed of a few guys from every grade. We were given some guidelines and materials, but we had free rein to decide which work of Poe we would present and how we would present it. On the third afternoon, we'd present our projects in the auditorium. Each presentation, which would be 5–15 minutes long, had to be done in good taste.

My group got to work brainstorming as soon as we arrived in our assigned room. Two other freshmen and I slid into our seats and remained silent as the upperclassmen shared ideas. The consensus was to steer away from the obvious choices like "The Raven" and "The Masque of the Red Death." They argued a little but finally decided on a presentation of "The Tell-Tale Heart." We took turns reading the entire story and then a summary version. A few guys wanted to do a serious rendition of the story, but it seemed best to go for some type of parody. One of the sophomores in our group, Malcolm, said we should really exaggerate the murdered guy's eye. He said he could paint a tennis ball and make it look really disgusting and bloody. I was so wrapped up in his description that I forgot my shyness.

"Hey, what if his whole head was an eyeball? Kinda like an alien version of the guy."

Instead of getting mad, Malcolm jumped up out of his seat. "Now you're talkin', man. I hope there's some kind of prize for this because we're going to blow the crowd away!"

We were totally prepared for show day. Numbers were drawn for the order of presentation, and we drew seventh out of fifteen groups. The student body sat through three versions of "The Raven" (only the serious version was good), two hilarious presentations of "The Masque of the Red Death" (one of which was Brandon's group), and a totally boring adaptation of "The Pit and the Pendulum" (that group used a swinging map of China as the pendulum . . . it was meant to be some type of political statement that no one quite understood).

Our presentation followed the China debacle. Since there were only five actual parts: the mad killer, the murdered eyeball, two police officers, and a narrator, most of us were off the hook for actually performing. The five guys who volunteered to do the acting were real stage hams. When Scott, who played the eyeball, walked on stage with Malcolm's creation, we had to stop until the laughter and hooting from the audience died down. Malcolm had used chicken wire, duct tape, tissue paper, and lots of red gooey stuff for his masterpiece. He created an eyeball that was the size of those big red balls that sit outside of Target. Scott had to use both of his hands to hold it steady.

The time came for the mad guy (played by Alex) to kill the man/eyeball. Alex pulled out a fountain pen. We had been smart enough to use suspenseful music and great sound effects. Malcolm had rigged a water balloon in the cornea of the eye, so when the actual stabbing occurred, water squirted from the eyeball and all over Alex. The combined effect had the auditorium going crazy!

No one remembers the rest of our parody. All anyone would talk about for weeks later was Malcolm's cool creation.

Our presentation was considered by many to be the highlight of the afternoon. I was certainly pleased, since I felt I made a good contribution. But, for me, the best part of the show was the very last performance.

The teachers asked some of the theater and drama students to recite excerpts of some of Poe's poems and plays. They wanted to end the day with a more accurate portrayal of Poe's work.

Dan Fisher, a junior classman, took the stage in period clothing. A gray tombstone chiseled with the name "Annabel Lee" was his only prop. He recited the words of Poe's famous poem by heart, from his heart. With the one stage light on him and the headstone, his voice whispered the words of the poem and hypnotized the audience.

But our love it was stronger by far than the love
Of those who were older than we—
Of many far wiser than we—
And neither the angels in heaven above,
Nor the demons down under the sea,
Can ever dissever my soul from the soul
Of the beautiful Annabel Lee.

The entire audience gave him a standing ovation. I could barely hold back tears; I felt one with Poe and his grief over his young bride. I understood completely the struggle of life when the one you love is gone. Once again, poetry was the conduit for my feelings.

The lights stayed dimmed, for which I was extremely grateful, and our principal gave his kudos to the teachers and the students for a wonderful afternoon. I felt exhausted and was thankful that it was Friday.

Chapter 28

HALLOWEEN was not the only event at the end of October. It also marked the end of our first quarter grading period; report cards would be issued in the first week of November. Because our school schedules miraculously synced, Brandon, I, and my mom would all have a short break together.

Brandon had a hockey tournament in Buffalo, New York, the weekend of our school break. Mom was excited about planning a weekend trip. We would leave Friday and return Sunday, and we still had Monday off. Dad's work schedule was flexible, so he was okay with leaving Friday.

Mom knew we needed a nice vacation. She booked a great hotel with an indoor pool and researched things to do in the area. I was happy about it too. The trip meant a lot less free time for me, and I enjoyed most of Brandon's tournaments.

The tournaments always involved a whole group of people that my mom referred to as our "hockey family." They were kids and parents who had been part of the same league for almost ten years.

We had some great times on the weekend tournaments. Most of the hotels we booked gave the team a party room. In the evenings we ate and socialized there. A table would be set up as a big buffet. It was arranged with an assortment of take-out or hotel food, a variety of hard and soft drinks, and hundreds of homemade cookies and snacks. There was always someone my age to hang out with, and even my dad enjoyed himself.

But, and I quote one of my dad's favorite lines, "the best laid plans of mice and men . . ." The Thursday before our trip, I awoke in the middle of the night in a somewhat delirious state. In my dream world, I envisioned these odd creatures who had thick heavy arms and legs. I looked at them, but I was also one of them. My body felt like it was moving in an atmosphere of Jell-O. Then a tree . . . that terrible tree with the teddy bear and the notes . . . was in front of me. Its branches became hands that were trying to grab me. I tried to run away, but at the same time, I needed to find Jessie and save her. But, my arms and my legs felt so heavy, and every movement was difficult and painful. I was trying to speak, but my mouth wouldn't form the words. I tried to call for Jessie. I knew there was something important I needed to tell her. But then, I could hear my mom; her voice sounded distant and garbled.

"Leo, Leo, what's wrong, honey?" And then, "Oh, sweetie, you're burning up."

Flu season had made its debut at North Central last week, and, lucky me, I got it just before my vacation and family trip were about to begin.

My mom called Grandma Lily in the morning so that she could take care of me, and then she called school to say I would be absent. Grandma stayed with me all day and brought me plenty of liquids to keep me hydrated.

Mom called my doctor while she was at work and picked up a prescription on her way home.

When she got home, Mom came directly to my room. She sat on the edge of my bed and pushed some locks of my hair off my forehead. She looked worried and upset.

"Looks like you'll be bedridden for at least a week, Leo. You're going to need plenty of TLC in the next few days, so I'm staying home with you. Dad and Brandon should be okay in Buffalo without us."

I tried to protest. I even suggested that Grandma Lily stay with me. But, for some strange reason, my mom seemed intent on staying with me. It was odd because she loved those trips with the team. She knew the worst was probably over, and I could take care of myself.

"Sometimes only a mother's love will work, Leo. I think that's what you need, sweetie. Now get some rest. I'll check on you in a few minutes."

Brandon and my dad left for Buffalo early the next morning. They stood by the door and waved. Both were afraid of getting sick themselves. Dad said he would call, and he promised to bring me something from Buffalo. I barely remember the rest of the day. Mom woke me to give me my medicine and make me drink something, but I slept through much of the next thirty-six hours.

Early Saturday morning I was feeling a little better. Mom coaxed me into eating. She brought a little bed tray into my room and set it on my lap. She had prepared a piece of toast, a small glass of orange juice, and a cup of hot tea for me. After she fluffed my pillows and made sure I was comfortable, she smiled and said she was glad I felt better. From my desk chair, she watched me eat and told me a little about her morning phone conversation with Dad and Brandon. When she could see that I had finished, she took the tray, set it on my desk, and sat down beside me. She grabbed both my hands and held them tightly in hers.

"Leo," she began, "since you were just a little baby, you've been like a perfect child. I can still remember your first day of kindergarten. I was so worried about getting two kids and myself ready for school every morning. Things are so hectic, and there never seems to be enough time in the morning. I remember getting up earlier than usual that first day. I figured I'd get myself ready, and then wake you and Brandon. I went to Brandon's room and just about dragged him, half asleep, to the bathroom. I took a damp cloth and wiped his face to wake him up, loaded up his toothbrush with paste, and then put the brush in his hand. When I felt he was sufficiently awake, I made my way to your room, ready to repeat the process. But, there you were, completely dressed, rummaging through your backpack."

She looked down at my hands and hers and then stared me in the eyes. She looked and sounded sad. This wasn't her usual tone when she reminisced about my childhood days.

"What I'm trying to say, sweetie, is that I've been a bad parent to you. You made everything so easy because you are such a responsible child and young man. I let myself believe that you can handle anything. I only nag you about things because I'm used to doing that with Brandon. But you are so organized and reliable. You get your homework done, you do your chores around here, and I never worry about the friends you hang out with."

I was staring at her, waiting for the hammer to fall. I thought maybe she'd seen my grades or gotten a bad report from my teachers when she called in my absence. My confidence about being a high honor student for this quarter was quickly waning.

"Sweetie, the other night, when you were feverish . . . well, what brought me into your room was that I heard you talking in your sleep. You know I'm a light sleeper, and you were actually talking and . . . and sobbing."

I held my breath. I wasn't ready for what she was about to say. I'd hid my feelings all this while only to have them revealed while I was delirious and asleep.

"Mom, . . . please . . ." My eyes were starting to fill up with tears. I could hardly make out her face, but I knew she was crying too.

"No, Leo," she said rather sternly, "you are not going to pretend that you're okay anymore. You need someone to talk to, and if it's not me, then I'm going to make sure it is someone else."

My mind was groggy and my voice was raspy. "I don't remember, Mom. It was just a bad dream. It was probably just the fever. I don't even know what I said."

"You were crying . . . you kept repeating 'I'm so sorry, Jesse. I love you, Jessie. I'm so sorry.' Then you looked like you were trying to say something, but you couldn't seem to form any more words. You opened your eyes, and, I can't exactly explain it, but it was like you were looking at something on the ceiling. It really scared me, Leo. I don't think I've ever felt so helpless around you."

I shook my head. I wanted to wipe some of my tears away, but she still gripped my hands.

"When we took you to the psychologist right after the accident, she told us that you seemed to have the right kind of coping mechanisms in play. But, she did tell us to be watchful for a delayed reaction to what happened. Your voice . . . while you were sleeping . . . well, Leo, . . . it broke my heart. I can't even describe how pained you sounded."

She took a deep breath and let out a long sigh. She turned her head away from me for a few seconds. I knew she was trying to compose her thoughts. When she looked back at me, tears slid down her cheeks.

"Leo, you need to talk to someone about what happened to you . . . what happened to Jessie. I was wrong in letting it go this far. You've had to deal with so much. I don't think you were ready to talk so soon after the accident, but it is something you have to do. We'll find you a grief counselor, someone who might understand what you're going through, someone who is easy for you to talk to."

I knew she was right. I needed to unburden myself to someone, but I wasn't quite sure I could share my feelings. As if she read my mind, my mom continued.

"You're so much like your father, Leo. Sharing your feelings isn't an easy thing for you. I know that. But, it's got to be much easier than enduring all your pain alone."

"I don't know if I can. I'm afraid, Mom, . . . there's so much I can't explain."

"Sweetie, I know you're still fighting this flu, so I'm going to give you time to heal physically. But, I'm going to make you an appointment to see a grief counselor. I'll make it for the middle of November. I'll go with you if you want. But you need to talk."

I just nodded. I felt relief and dread at the same time. She let go of my hands and wrapped her arms around me. We hugged for a long time; both of us cried. When she finally let go, she wiped away some of my tears and kissed me on the forehead. Then, just as she used to do when she tucked me into bed when I was little, she traced a little cross on my forehead.

"I love you so much, Leo."

Chapter 29

DAD AND BRANDON RETURNED from Buffalo and eagerly shared the events of the weekend. Brandon brought me a tournament shirt from his team, and Dad bought me a Buffalo Bills hoodie. They were excited and happy. Brandon's team won first place against a Canadian team in the finals.

My dad gave us a play-by-play description of the last period. He was just as excited about the win as Brandon. I sensed his eyes watching my reactions when he talked. It wasn't hard to figure out that Mom had filled him in about our weekend events.

Later that evening, he came into my room. I sat in bed with a book propped on my lap.

"Glad to see you're feeling better, Leo. You still need to rest though, so make sure you're getting enough sleep."

He walked to the window in my room and drew back the drape. He kept his eyes on the night sky.

"Sharing sadness with others isn't easy, and it isn't going to make all the hurt go away," he said, almost to himself. "But, it does help."

His hand let go of the drape, and then he turned and walked to my bed. He touched the corner of my shoulder and then tousled my hair.

"Don't think that you have to be strong, Leo. You have us to lean on."

He said goodnight and walked into the hallway. I felt weak and exhausted. I put my book on the nightstand, turned out my light, and fell asleep quickly.

When Mom and Brandon returned to school on Tuesday, Brandon was recruited to get schoolwork from my teachers. I was grateful on two levels: I was able to keep up with my assignments and not have a ton of makeup work to do on my return, and also the work helped fill some empty hours.

Grandma Lily volunteered to stay with me during the day. She came early in the morning and made sure I was fed and hydrated. Most of the time, I went downstairs in the morning and made myself comfortable on the sofa in the family room. I enjoyed watching some old television shows between naps, and my Grandma Lily filled the house with distracting noises. The whirr of the vacuum, the hum of the dryer, or the clatter of kitchen utensils kept my mind drawn to the mundane.

In the afternoon I completed my assignments. None of them were taxing, and I usually finished my work in an hour. Luckily, since this was the start of a new quarter, I was not missing any major tests.

My strength slowly returned, and my naps grew more infrequent. By the end of that week, the doctor gave me the okay to return to school.

My return to good health meant that we had adjustments to make. My family had quickly grown accustomed to Grandma Lily's presence in the house. My parents loved coming home to a clean house, a freshly baked pie or cake, and dinner ready to go into the oven. Brandon enjoyed having a clean room and freshly laundered and ironed clothes. And I, I had to reacquaint myself with my alarm clock and get through the school day without a nap.

True to her word, Mom made some phone calls and located someone who was considered one of the best grief counselors in the area. Mrs. Franco specialized in teen grief, and her office was located just two blocks from North Central. Mom spoke to her on the phone, and they agreed to schedule six sessions, two each week, for the next three weeks. Then, my parents, Mrs. Franco, and I would meet and assess my progress, and we would make a group decision as to what was needed after that.

My first appointment was for a Tuesday in the middle of November. Since I could walk to Mrs. Franco's office after school, my dad volunteered to be in charge of picking me up. It was his way of showing me support, since words that dealt with emotions didn't come easy to him.

Nonetheless, my dad had an important place in my memories of Jessie's death. The days of bereavement after Jessie died are a blur in my mind. Some things, though, are like photographs in my mind. Many of those stored pictures focus on my dad.

He was at my side at the funeral parlor; I felt him physically supporting the weight of my body as he and Mom walked me to the coffin. He put his arm around me as we sat with Jessie's parents and watched other mourners come and go. He gave people a look when they approached me . . . a stay-away, he's not ready to talk, kind of look. And of the few things I remember about the funeral service—Jessie's parents looking numb and exhausted, the awful sobbing coming from friends, the overwhelming smell of hundreds of flowers—the one thing that touched me to the core was the tears that streamed from my dad's eyes.

I had never seen him cry before. I knew his tears were for me as much as for Jessie.

I know my father loves me
I see it in his eyes
Though words he does not utter
In his heart is where love lies

Only Jessie's parents were at her internment; she was buried in Erie, Pennsylvania. Mr. Delaney said that was where his family cemetery plots were located. So, I had to just watch as Jessie's steel blue coffin was lifted into the hearse. The finality of her death slammed into my heart when the hatch door closed and the hearse pulled away. My brother and my father stood at each side of me and helped me to our car.

The ride home was long. My mom drove, and my brother sat in front. My dad and I sat in the back. He held his arm around my shoulder the entire ride home.

"I'm here for you, Leo," he whispered, "I'm here for you."

I only stared out the window. I felt such emptiness. Even though I appreciated my family's support, I wanted nothing more than to be left alone with my grief.

Chapter 30

WHEN THE TUESDAY of my appointment with the grief counselor arrived, the school day flew by. I thought about feigning some illness or just catching the bus home and saying I forgot, but I knew that wouldn't work. It would do me no good to avoid the inevitable. But, my heart was not ready to dredge up all the things I tried so hard to conceal.

I made it to the counseling center about ten minutes before my appointment. After entering the reception area, I walked up to the receptionist, gave my name, and headed for the magazine rack. The *Highlights* magazine beckoned me; the hunt for hidden objects would detour my mind from more serious thoughts. But, I did not even get to sit down before the receptionist called my name.

"Mrs. Franco will see you now. Just go through the door and down the hall to the right."

Mrs. Franco met me at her office door. She was very petite—I was at least a head taller than she. After my summer growth spurt, I was now at five foot, eleven inches and one of the tallest freshmen at North Central.

She reached out and shook my hand. She smiled at me, more with her dark eyes than with her mouth.

"I'm Mrs. Franco, Lee. Come on in and sit down. At least then I can look you in the eye."

We sat across from each other in soft leather chairs. Mrs. Franco didn't look as small anymore. She wore some casual black slacks and a pastel pink sweater. I guessed she was about my mom's age or older. She didn't have any kind of notebook or writing materials. Only a small coffee table with some magazines, a pitcher of water, and some glasses was between us.

"Would you care for something to drink, Lee? I can get you a soft drink if you don't want water."

"No, thank you, ma'am. I'm fine."

She nodded in reply and then continued. "This is just a little get-acquainted session, Lee. I'm going to give you an idea of who I am and how I operate. Your mom and I talked, so I have some background on you. And, Lee, I'm not going to force you to talk to me. What I want to do is help you . . . help you in any way I can. If that means suggesting some ways for you to cope with your pain, then that's what I'll do."

I nodded as if to say that's fine. I couldn't look at her directly, so I played with a little frayed piece of thread on the corner of the leather seat of my chair.

"First, I want to express my sincere sympathy to you. You've lost a friend, someone you loved deeply. On top of that you have the tragedy of witnessing her death. All of that is a great burden to bear. I would never and will never say that I understand what you are going through. No one does. Your pain is not like anyone else's, so the way you deal with that pain is a process only you can figure out."

Her voice was firm; her words seemed sincere. She took a deep breath and audibly sighed. I instinctively did the same. It was a relief to hear someone acknowledge my pain, especially when I didn't feel the need to say anything in return.

"Your parents told me what a smart young man you are. I'm not going to bore you with a review of the stages of grief. You're not here to listen to a lecture. So let me tell you what I know already . . . some things that your mom has shared."

My body relaxed. It felt good to be off the hook about talking and sharing. I knew that wouldn't last forever, but, for now, I could just listen.

Apparently my mother had more than one short conversation with Mrs. Franco. Without any notes or other references, she summarized the events that brought me to a grief counselor. She was factual, but there was understanding and sympathy in her voice.

I nodded as I listened. Nothing she said was wrong. She had my story as my parents knew it. I, of course, knew so many missing elements. It was this gape in my story that made me feel so isolated and so distant from God. These were the things that I found difficult to share; the things gnawing at my soul.

"Lee, if you don't mind, I'd like to ask you a few questions. If you don't feel like answering any of them, that's your decision. But I hope you know that you can trust me."

My body stiffened. I waited for the questions that would try to stir up my feelings about the accident or ask me to express my feelings of loss.

"I'm wondering if you'd tell me a little about yourself. What kind of student are you? What are your favorite school subjects? Do you play any sports? You know, the kinds of things that might help me know you better."

I hadn't expected such trivial little questions, and it was rather relaxing to talk about golf and some of my classes and teachers. I even shared with her that I liked to write. It felt just like a regular conversation, not like a therapy session. She shared with me that her two brothers had attended North Central, too. Her brothers hadn't played any sports, but they were both on the school newspaper and the yearbook committee.

When our time was almost up, Mrs. Franco stood, and I did the same.

"You're quite an interesting young man, Lee. I look forward to our next meeting and hope that you do too."

I smiled and thanked her.

"I do have one little thing I'd like you to do between now and Thursday. Since you're a writer, I want you to keep a little journal of your thoughts . . . good or bad, sentences or just words. It's nothing you have to share with me, unless of course that's what you'd like to do. I'd like you to do that for the entire three weeks. You can write as often as you like, but try to make at least one entry each day."

Half-heartedly, I agreed. We walked together to the reception area, and I thanked her again. The receptionist gave me a card reminding me to be back on Thursday at the same time.

I checked my phone. My dad had texted me that he was waiting across the street.

My dad and I have a good rapport, and the ride home was quiet and relaxing. He never pushes me into talking about my feelings. He knew I would share when I was ready. We talked about school a little, but mostly we just looked out at the already darkened landscape and listened to the radio.

Mom had dinner waiting for us, even though it was only five o'clock. But Brandon had hockey practice, and an early dinner usually worked for everyone. We just talked about general things as we ate, and no one asked me any questions about my appointment.

Dad decided to drive Brandon to his practice, and Mom and I cleaned up the dishes.

"Everything go alright with your appointment today, Leo?" she said almost too casually. I knew she wanted a full transcript of my session, but she was afraid I would clam up if she asked too much.

"Yeah, Mrs. Franco seemed really nice . . . ya know, easy to talk to."

"You're okay then . . . I mean about going back again on Thursday?"

"Sure, Mom, I'll finish all the sessions. Don't worry so much."

She seemed relieved and gave me a hug. "I'll finish up here. Relax and get your homework done."

My assignments didn't take long, so I watched some television and got ready for bed. I pulled out a notebook and wrote down some of my thoughts about the day. I wrote about my dad and mom mostly; how important it was for me to know how much they cared. Then, I did something I hadn't done since Jessie died. I wrote a poem.

Your hair, your face, your jade green eyes,
Your skin, your lips, your words so wise,
The way you touched my heart, my soul,
The way you made my life so whole.
What can I do to fill this space?
No one, no love will ever replace
This need I have for your embrace.

I closed the notebook and placed it in my nightstand drawer. It felt good to write again, especially to write about Jessie. My alarm clock showed 9:58. I walked slowly to the window and looked out at our backyard. A few light snow flakes started to fall, and our grass had a crystal glaze. No stars were visible, and I could barely make out the hazy shadow of a half moon.

I turned and looked at my clock. When it turned to ten o'clock, I whispered to the sky, "I love you, Jessie. I miss you, Jessie. I'm so sorry, Jessie." The same words I said every night since Jessie died.

Chapter 31

CHRISTMAS DECORATIONS go up early in the Harrison house. The Monday after Thanksgiving, Mom ordered me and Brandon to pull the Christmas boxes from the garage and attic. Our annual Thanksgiving trip to see my grandparents in Ohio was done, and Mom was ready to be in the spirit of the season. Brandon and I moved furniture and placed boxes as Mom barked her orders. Then she blasted Christmas music as she lovingly decorated the house.

We were almost done, even with some outside decorations, when my dad came home from work. He had picked up some Chinese food for dinner, and we ate as soon as he came in the door.

We were all exhausted, especially Mom. So, after eating a dessert of ice cream and cookies, we all decided to call it a night. Dad volunteered to clean up the kitchen, and then he shooed us to bed. Mom, Brandon, and I didn't need any urging.

I showered, listened to a Penguin's hockey game on the radio, and pulled out my school planner to see if I had any important assignments due.

The next day was Tuesday, which meant my second-to-last session with Mrs. Franco.

I was pleased with our progress, and I was quite sure she would say I didn't need any more appointments. Our previous session had actually been very enjoyable. Mrs. Franco asked me about Jessie, and it was great to tell someone about her. Most everyone avoids mentioning her name around me.

For a while that was how I wanted it. But now, I needed to talk about her, to remember aloud some of the wonderful times we'd had together. My family and friends were still too nervous to bring her up in a conversation, and I wasn't comfortable enough to do that myself.

But, with Mrs. Franco, it was all a part of the process. She reminded me how important it was to talk about Jessie. It was a relief and a joy. I ached to tell someone about all the things that made Jessie so wonderful.

I decided to share some of Jessie's poems with Mrs. Franco. I made copies from some of our emails, and I put them in a blue folder. Mrs. Franco would see another side of Jessie. It was one I had tried to describe to her, but I knew the poems would reveal Jessie in a way that my words were not able. I even put Jessie's eighth grade school picture with the folder.

I held the 5x7 picture in my hand and smiled. Jessie looked so beautiful. The photo had captured the smile in her eyes and even the timid half-smile that always melted my heart. Her teal V-neck top revealed the butterfly necklace, my first gift to her.

I tucked the folder into my planner and then into my backpack. I imagined Mrs. Franco looking at the picture and reading the poems, and finally understanding some of the reasons why I felt so lost.

It was hard to get out of bed the next morning. After five days of Thanksgiving vacation, including our annual trip to Ohio, and all that eating, my body was in a stupor. I was glad I had phys ed class in my schedule. Exercise would wake me up and give me some energy.

The halls of North Central were relatively quiet that Tuesday morning as students made their way to homerooms. Everyone felt the way I did, and I knew the teachers would probably be dragging too. I stopped at my locker and picked up the books I needed for my morning classes. I made a pile of books and folders in the hallway and then hung up my backpack. The pile was enormous because my literature book and algebra book were huge.

I carried the stack to homeroom without any mishaps. But when I set the pile on my desk in the middle of the room, everything toppled over. Books plopped to the floor, and folders slid into the aisle. The blue folder with Jessie's picture and poems fell from my planner, and the contents spilled across the tiled floor. Most of the class heard the crash, but no one moved because they were either busy or disinterested.

I bent over and hurriedly began picking things up. Phil Knox, one of the biggest freshmen and a member of the junior varsity football team, sat in the next row of seats. He is not really a bully, but he is known as a tough guy with a big-man-on-campus attitude. Jessie's picture and several of her poems landed right by his feet. He picked up the papers and then Jessie's picture.

"Wow, Lee. Some hot chick you have here. She your sweetie?"

When I reached to take the pile from his hand, he held me at arm's length with his free hand. He turned his head toward the papers in his other hand.

"That's personal, Phil. Just give it to me, man." I tried to keep my voice cool. If I showed real desperation, he wouldn't let up.

His hand felt like it relaxed, and I waited for him to hand everything over. But instead, his voice level raised just enough for most of the class to hear.

"Slithering little caterpillar," he read in a girly, sing-songy voice.

My heart beat rapidly, and my eyes welled up with angry tears. He had no right to make fun of that poem, no right to even look at something that was Jessie's heart and soul!

"Not so pleasant to the eye," he continued in that disgusting falsetto.

I faintly heard people laughing in the background, and Mr. Simmons, my homeroom teacher, yelled for both of us to sit down.

"Soon, in a cocoon . . . ."

My right arm came out of nowhere, surprising Phil, and even surprising me. It made perfect contact with Phil's upper lip and part of his nose. He removed his left hand from my chest and dropped my papers from his right hand, quickly taking both hands to his face.

Blood gushed from his nose, and his eyes looked more startled than angry.

I scooped up the papers and began shoving them into my desk. Tears streamed down my eyes, and my heart raced so fast that I felt faint. Mr. Simmons ran over to Phil with some tissue. He stood as a blocker between the two of us.

"Office, Mr. Harrison. Immediately! Mr. Knox will be there too, after he sees the nurse."

Chapter 32

MISS WHILEY, our vice-principal, was a stern, commanding presence. Even the senior guys changed to respectful young men when she was in the room. Her rather petite size and matronly look took a backseat when she spoke. She was a drill sergeant who looked like a grandmother.

A small area that was visible from the hallway blocked any view of Miss Whiley's office. Mrs. Oliver, her secretary, occupied that space. Very few people ever got beyond the secretary's desk. Mrs. Oliver would either satisfy your problem, or you would wait in one of two chairs until Miss Whiley appeared.

Miss Whiley's inner office was a place made famous through urban legend. Rumors circulated about secret doors that held cattle prods and other torturing devices. No one I knew at North Central had ever even caught a glimpse of the room through an open door.

Now I sat alone in that office. I didn't even remember walking through the hallway. My highly emotional state was replaced with exhaustion. I just wanted to go home and slide under my covers. I looked around the room in an attempt to distract myself from the whispering voices outside.

Family pictures, neatly stacked folders, and a bobblehead of Tiger Woods sat on Miss Whiley's enormous desk. The wall behind her desk was covered with diplomas and plaques. The remaining walls were adorned with a collection of sports memorabilia from various Dragon teams of North Central.

The lack of torture tools did not ease my fears. North Central has a very strict policy about physical violence and bullying. Several days during the first few weeks of school were dedicated to reviewing those policies. I knew I was facing suspension and possibly expulsion from school.

My thoughts were interrupted when the door pushed open and Miss Whiley entered her office.

"I've made some phone calls, Lee. Your father will be here shortly. This is a very serious situation you've put yourself in."

I kept silent and looked down at my hands. Miss Whiley would shoot down any explanation as an excuse. Besides, I couldn't really explain my actions to her.

She continued in a stern and angry voice. "Phil Knox is still with the nurse. His nose stopped bleeding, but his lip is swollen. We are going to let him sit there until his parents are contacted."

Oh, God, I thought. I had not even considered that I might have really hurt Phil. Maybe his parents would even sue. My days here at North Central were definitely numbered. My dad's face popped into my head. It would break his heart if I wouldn't graduate from North Central.

"Until your father arrives you will sit in an empty classroom. I'll have your books sent there with a list of work from some of the teachers. I suggest you compose your thoughts, too. You have quite a bit of explaining . . . and apologizing to do."

My isolation room was an unused science lab. Shortly after I sat down, Mr. Simmons arrived with my books and folders. He placed them on the science table where I sat.

"You okay, Lee?" he asked.

I was surprised by his caring voice. I anticipated anger and disappointment.

"I'm okay, sir. I'm sorry about my behavior. Thanks for bringing my things."

He placed his hand on my shoulder. "It will be okay, Lee. I can vouch for you if you need support."

I thanked him again, and he walked out of the room.

The blue folder sat neatly under my Algebra II book. My eyes watered as I recalled the incident that caused me to be here. I wondered if the photo and poem had been thrown in the trash. The last time I saw them they were a crumpled mess. I remembered shoving them into my desk after I hit Phil.

I slid the folder from under the textbook and anxiously opened it. The wrinkled paper and the other poems had been placed carefully into the right pocket. In the left pocket I saw the top part of Jessie's picture. I pulled out the photo, and Jessie's beautiful face stared at me. I traced my fingertip along the outline of her cheek.

What would you think of me now, Jessie?

At around 10:30 a voice came through the intercom in the science lab. I was told to report to the vice-principal's office.

Miss Whiley's secretary told me to go into her office. I knocked and entered. Miss Whiley was seated behind her desk, and my father and Mrs. Franco were in the chairs across from her.

My eyes went directly to the floor; I was not ready to face the disappointment in my dad's eyes.

"Have a seat, Leo," Miss Whiley said. Her voice was different now. It was the voice that teachers use when a parent is present.

The only seat available was between my dad and Mrs. Franco. I slid between them and sat down. Almost simultaneously they each placed a hand on my knees and gave me a reassuring squeeze. I could feel my dad's eyes, but I continued looking at the floor. It seemed like minutes of silence passed.

Miss Whiley was the first to break the silence. "Lee, Mr. Simmons spoke to your father and apprised him of the events that occurred this morning in homeroom. Since Mrs. Franco was close by and available, your father asked her to sit in on this meeting."

My anger and embarrassment rose inside me again. This was the last thing I wanted. I did not need my problems and tragedies aired at school. This was supposed to be a place where I could just pretend to be a normal kid, not the kid with the dead girlfriend who was seeing a psychologist.

Mrs. Franco spoke up. "Lee, your father told Miss Whiley some of the reasons why you might have lost your temper today. I have shared nothing. I am only here to listen and offer any help that you might request from me."

This was her way of saying that she would not reveal anything that I had told her at our sessions. That gave me some relief, but I was still wary of what was happening.

Miss Whiley continued. "I have had a long conversation with Phil Knox and his mother. Phil admitted he was out of line with what he did. He also admitted that he physically pushed you, and even though punching him in the face was not a correct response, he understands why you became angry. He and his mom agreed to allow the school to evaluate a punishment for both of you."

My dad finally spoke, but he directed his comments only to me. "Leo, I know that the only people at school who knew about the tragedy that happened in August were Brandon, a few of his friends, and your golf coach. But, as much as I understand your need for privacy, I needed to inform Miss Whiley and Mr. Simmons, so that they could get a sense of why you reacted as you did. I also told Miss Whiley about your seeing Mrs. Franco—that you are in a process of dealing with your grief."

Miss Whiley interjected in a business-like voice. "Yes, Lee. No one is condoning your actions. But, many factors have to be considered. Mr. Simmons has already attested to your good character. Your father has assured me that you will continue to see Mrs. Franco for as long as necessary. And, of course, knowing the tragic events that have transpired in your young life . . . well, I am going to recommend to Principal Magnella that you have a one-day suspension. We would consider today as that suspension. That would allow you to return to school tomorrow. Also, before school opens tomorrow, I'm asking you to sit down with Phil and Father Michael so you can clear the air before going to classes. Father Michael can meet with both of you at seven."

My father began to speak. "Thank you, Miss Whiley, that sounds completely acceptable to . . ."

"No . . . no . . ." My words interrupted my dad, and he turned with a puzzled look.

"I don't need or want special treatment. I hit someone! Most kids get at least a week of suspension for that." My voice was louder than I intended it to be. In a much softer tone, I finished my plea. "I should be punished . . . I need to be punished . . . just like any other student."

I wiped away a few tears that had trickled down my cheek. Miss Whiley looked at my dad; my dad looked at me. We froze in time for a few seconds like some cartoon version of life.

Mrs. Franco spoke firmly to all of us. "Please, everyone, may I say something?"

My father and Miss Whiley nodded. They looked relieved that she was taking the helm.

"As much as we are all trying to help Lee—because obviously that's what we're trying to do —no one has really given him a chance to speak for himself. If there is one thing that I have learned about him, it's that he is an intelligent, capable young man. Yes, he's had a great tragedy in his life. Jessie's death changed him . . . the loss of someone you love always changes you . . . but he needs to, and he wants to, learn to deal with that. Treating him like a helpless child isn't helping him to cope."

Mrs. Franco still didn't have it right, but she at least supported my need to take ownership of what I had done. Mrs. Franco took everyone's continued silence as agreement.

"So, let me suggest that Lee and I go over to my office. We can walk over together or Mr. Harrison can drop him off. Instead of our usual afternoon appointment, I can see Lee now."

She looked at me for my assent and then continued. "When we're done, you can call your dad, Lee, and he can take you home for the rest of the day."

I nodded in agreement. Mrs. Franco was the one person I thought I could talk to right now.

"Miss Whiley, what is the usual punishment for a first offense of fighting here at North Central?" Mrs. Franco was obviously in charge of this meeting now.

"Well," Miss Whiley began, "it is typically three to five days, depending on the amount of violence involved."

"Then I'm sure Lee and his father would consider it kind of you to give him three days."

My father actually looked like he was smiling at this point. Mrs. Franco's style was winning him over, and although she just negotiated a longer punishment for me, he knew it was fair.

"Okay then, Lee—three days, and I will talk to Father Michael about rescheduling your meeting with Phil to seven on Friday morning." Miss Whiley looked a little confused by what just progressed, but she was handling it like a pro.

I regained some composure, and I thanked Miss Whiley and apologized once again for my behavior. She stood up and escorted us to the door. Miss Whiley's secretary was not in the outer office.

My father spoke to Mrs. Franco as soon as Miss Whiley closed her office door. "Mrs. Franco, I cannot express enough gratitude. It is obvious to me that you understand Leo better than I do. I'd like a moment with him, and then I can take both of you to your office."

"Sometimes love blinds our ability to see the people who are close to us. Your instinct is to protect your son. You have no reason to apologize for that. You two take all the time you need. I can use a good walk. Just drop Lee off at my building. I'll tell my receptionist he'll be coming. We have a nice cafeteria in the building. You can get some coffee and something to eat while you are waiting. I'd like to be able to talk with Lee for about an hour."

She grabbed her coat from the coat rack, gave us a quick smile, and walked down the hallway. As soon as we were totally alone, Dad grabbed me and hugged me tight.

"You *are* a smart young man, Leo . . . smart enough to know that I love you, and I would do anything to help you through this. But, sometimes you need to let other people help you. You're not alone with this. Sometimes sharing is what you need to do to lessen your pain. You know I'm not the best talker, but I am a good listener."

"I know, Dad, I know. It's just . . . it's not easy for me to talk about all the things I need to talk about."

"Well," he said with a smile, "you are your father's son."

We picked up my books from the science lab and got some things from my locker. My dad and I drove the short distance to the Pittsburgh Behavioral Health Building where Mrs. Franco's office was located. Dad waited in the cafeteria. He had his laptop and could do some of his work.

The receptionist escorted me to Mrs. Franco's office. Juice and bagels were on the coffee table, and she told me to eat something while I waited. Mrs. Franco needed to complete some paperwork and make a phone call before she would join me.

I was hungry and helped myself to a cinnamon bagel. I wondered whether we would be addressing today's incident or just continue with my grief counseling. The blue folder was in my dad's car, so I wouldn't be able to share Jessie's poems with Mrs. Franco today. It was probably better that way. I needed to forget about my hurt, embarrassment, and anger over what Phil had done.

Mrs. Franco entered just as I poured my second glass of cranberry juice.

"Have some more, Lee. I can wait until you're finished." She sat down opposite me. For the first time since we started our sessions, she held a clipboard and some paper.

I sipped a little bit of juice and then set my glass back on the table between us.

"I'm finished, thanks." Suddenly I felt apprehensive.

Mrs. Franco looked more pensive than usual, and she seemed hesitant about beginning our session.

Mrs. Franco had managed to become important to me in just the few weeks I'd known her. She had an ability to display an understanding of my feelings without ever saying anything. I talked and even laughed about my times with Jessie, and she never belittled my feelings. So, I felt that I owed her more than my usual mediocre effort. I began with an apology.

"Mrs. Franco, I know I really messed up your day . . . you know, the meeting this morning and now this early meeting. Well . . . what I'm trying to say is . . . if you don't have time to meet with me now, I'm sure I can wait until Thursday."

Mrs. Franco placed the clipboard onto the table and scooted up to the edge of her chair. She leaned forward and looked me in the eyes.

"You didn't mess up my day, Lee. What happened today at North Central was an inevitable event. What I'm trying to do is just sort out where we need to go from here."

"An inevitable event? . . . You mean you knew I would hit someone?"

"No, Lee, that's not what I'm saying. What happened was just your mind's way of getting out the anger and hurt you've been feeling. Sometimes mental issues show themselves in physical ways. I know what precipitated the punch. Mr. Simmons told your father and me about the poem and the picture of Jessie. Your classmate was teasing you about things that are very important to you. Since he and your other classmates don't know about Jessie's death, he really didn't understand how hurtful he was being."

"I really didn't mean to hit him so hard. Honestly, I don't even remember doing it."

"That's just part of the issue, Lee. You've been sharing quite a bit with me during our four sessions together, but . . . you know you have never actually spoken about the day that Jessie died. I know your parents were present when the police questioned you, but as far as I know, that was the only time you spoke about the actual event."

I started to get angry. "I told them everything. Why would I need to repeat it to anyone else?" That day was always with me. I didn't need or want to describe the details to anyone.

"Lee, you are carrying the burden of that day on your shoulders. You need to share that heavy load with someone."

She picked up her clipboard and scanned a few pages. I could see that they were handwritten notes.

"Let me share with you some things that are troubling me. Maybe you'll understand my concern. First, the reason you are here is because your mother was worried after she discovered you crying in your sleep. She said that you kept repeating "I'm sorry . . . Jessie, I'm so sorry . . ." When we were with Miss Whiley, you expressed a need to be punished."

I interrupted, and I surprised myself with the anger in my voice. "I was talking about the punishment for hitting Phil . . . that's what I was talking about. And the dream—I don't even remember what that was about!"

"Lee, let me finish. Most people have guilt about something when someone they love dies. It might be about the last few things they said, or that they should have been nicer, or they should have been able to prevent the death. There is no shame in that guilt, but it is a guilt most adults can't carry on their own. You need to talk about what you really felt on the day Jessie died. You can't keep hiding your emotions from people who love you and want to help you."

My back stiffened, I squeezed my eyes tightly shut, and I took a deep painful breath. I was having difficulty controlling my rage.

"I can't talk about it! The words won't come out. It's too hard for me. I know I can't get through the whole story. It's too hard."

I fought the tears and fought the emotions inside me. Part of me wanted Mrs. Franco to say, "Okay, someday you'll be ready," and the other part of me needed her to ask me the perfect question that would unleash my story.

Mrs. Franco ignored my display of temper and calmly continued. "Lee, we've got to come up with a plan that you can handle. I told you on our first session that I would never force you to talk. But, your response just now tells me that you want to talk. You just don't know how."

I relaxed my face and my shoulders. My eyes and my hands remained tightly closed.

"Let me make two suggestions, and you pick the one that you feel you can best handle. Or, maybe you have an idea of your own."

I nodded slightly and opened my eyes.

"First suggestion. We could determine together what part of the day of Jessie's death you would talk about. So, instead of thinking about the whole day, you could, in our next session, tell me about the things you were doing just before the accident. That way you'd feel less pressure. It would be a first step. Then the next session we would talk about the actual accident and what you witnessed."

I just shrugged. Mrs. Franco didn't understand that the time before the accident would be just as difficult as the accident itself. Although this felt almost possible, it would still be difficult.

"Well, think about that idea. It's the same philosophy that I used when doing a long and difficult assignment in school. I found that breaking it up into small parts made it an easier thing to do."

I shrugged again. What would her other option be? I wondered if hypnotism was going to be the other choice, and I knew that option would not appeal to me at all.

"Okay, Lee, my other suggestion is based on what I know about you. You like to write, and you are a good writer. So, what if you would type out your story. You have three days of suspension, and I know you'll have schoolwork to complete too, but you could get everything out of your system at your own pace. And, it's not like it's a graded assignment. You needn't worry about grammar. You don't even have to talk about your feelings. Just put down on paper what happened that day."

My eyes widened as I contemplated writing down my story. It made sense. My thoughts and feelings were always easier for me to share on paper. Hell, my whole relationship with Jessie was based on our mutual love of writing.

Mrs. Franco sensed my openness to this suggestion. She waited while I controlled myself enough to respond.

"I think I could do that, Mrs. Franco. I think the words would come out on paper much easier and better than if I tried to tell anyone."

"I'm glad to hear you say that, Lee. I want you to know it's for my eyes only. You won't have to share your story with anyone else."

We spent about another half hour talking about what happened at school that morning. Mrs. Franco asked me to think about what I wanted to share with Phil and Father Michael at our Friday morning meeting. She told me that telling Phil about Jessie could be a good thing. He needed to know why I reacted the way I did.

I wasn't so sure about that. I didn't want people asking me questions about Jessie, or worse, treating me differently. I told Mrs. Franco that I would give everything a lot of thought in the next few days. We had a scheduled meeting on Thursday at our regular time, so I only had a few days to decide my course of action.

Mrs. Franco walked me to the reception area. She reached out and put her hand on my elbow. Her diminutive size prevented her from touching my shoulder. She looked up at me and smiled.

"Lee, I firmly believe that everything happens for a purpose." Then she laughed, "So, I guess what I'm saying is that I'm glad you hit that kid today. He deserved it, and so did you." She laughed again and gave me a little wink.

I walked down the stairway to the cafeteria two floors below. Dad was sitting in a far corner table. His open laptop and a cup of coffee were in front of him. He had his cell phone to his ear, and he waved me over as soon as he saw me.

"Sure, I'll talk to you later. Leo is here now, so we'll be on our way home." He placed his cell down on the table and told me to have a seat.

"You want anything, Leo? They have a great assortment of sandwiches, or maybe you just want a good dessert."

"I'm fine, Dad," I said and sat down across from him.

"Are you really, Leo? . . . Fine, I mean. Your mom and I are very concerned about you. That was her on the phone. We're both at a loss as to what we should do. We don't expect to understand all the things you're going through, but we don't want you to shut us out."

"I know, Dad . . . I'm trying. Mrs. Franco and I had a good talk, and I think I understand that I have to talk more. It's just . . ." My voice faded off.

I wanted to let my dad know that it wasn't his fault. My misery shouldn't turn into everyone else's misery. But again, words just don't come out as easily as they form in my head. I didn't want to say something that would make matters worse, and I certainly didn't want my dad or mom to think that they were doing something wrong.

"Leo, all I can say is that I love you, and I'm proud of you. Nothing you say or don't say will ever change that."

Chapter 33

WE ARRIVED HOME only an hour before my mom. I changed my clothes and arranged my books and papers on top of my desk. I tucked the blue folder into my desk drawer. I still hoped to share it with Mrs. Franco, but I didn't even want to look at it now. I did some mundane tasks around my room; I made my bed, hung up some clothes from my floor, and arranged some collectibles on my shelves. Eventually I heard my mom's voice coming from downstairs. I knew that she and Dad needed to talk, and I dreaded facing her. I didn't anticipate any anger, but I was not in the mood for a tearful or emotional talk. I was just too exhausted.

The knock on my door came much later than I expected. My parents had plenty to talk about, and I imagined them trying to figure out a plan of action.

"Come in," I said in a somewhat welcoming tone.

To my surprise it was Brandon's face that pushed into the door opening.

"Hey, bro, how's it going?" He didn't wait for a response. He opened the door and sat at my desk. I sat on the edge of my bed.

"I heard what happened at school today. Wow! My little brother popping big Phil Knox right on the nose. Didn't know you had it in you, Leo."

I gave my usual response, a shrug and a nod.

"Miss Whiley came and got me at the end of the day. She gave me some assignments from your teachers, and some official-looking envelope for Mom and Dad. Heard you got a three-day suspension. You should be glad you didn't get expelled. They gave Phil a one-day. I guess they figured a bloody nose and a fat lip were part of his punishment." Brandon made a boxing jab with his hand and laughed.

I was ready to jump in and brag about my hit, but that would have been a diversion to keep Brandon from understanding what I really felt. My dad's and Mrs. Franco's plea to talk and not shut people out repeated in my head.

"I really shouldn't have hit him, Brandon. Phil's not a bad guy—just a jerk."

Brandon's expression changed from amused to concerned.

"Yeah, Leo, he is a jerk . . . and . . . I know why you hit him. Dad talked to me and told me about the picture of Jessie. Phil was just teasing you because it was a girl's picture. He didn't know . . . well, you know . . . he didn't know Jessie died."

"Do any of the other guys at school know about the fight?"

"Well, sure, Leo. You know how quickly news like that spreads. Guys are worse than girls about spreading gossip, especially when it's about a fight."

"What about Jessie? Does anyone know about me and Jessie?" I kept my voice calm, but I really needed to know what was going on at school.

Brandon started to answer and then stopped. He was trying to read whether or not I was ready for what he was about to say.

"Leo, I think you should prepare yourself before going back to school on Friday. There was a lot of talk about the fight, and a lot of the guys in your homeroom were telling different versions of what happened. And, well, Jeff . . . Jeff just couldn't keep his mouth shut. He was defending you, and well . . . he told some of the guys about what happened to Jessie. This is the first time he said anything, I swear. I told him before school even started that you didn't seem to want anyone to know. He was really cool with that. But, Leo, he wanted to let the guys know what made you mad enough to hit someone."

Jeff was Brandon's best friend at school. They played football together this year and spent a lot of time together during the school day. I couldn't be angry with him for trying to help me.

"It's okay, Brandon. It had to come out sometime. It's probably better coming from someone like you or Jeff, rather than someone who doesn't know me at all."

"Leo, once word spread, most of the guys felt bad for you and even for Phil. I think you'll see that they might treat you different for a while, but they'll relax around you soon enough. Honestly, I think this is better for you. All the guys sensed that something wasn't right . . . you always seem like you don't want to have a good time. Like you're too serious. There are a lot of good guys at school. You've got to trust other people to understand some of the things you're feeling."

At that last statement, I started to feel a surge of anger build in me again. How could those guys at school really understand my feelings? My anger lessened as I reminded myself that Brandon was making an effort to help me.

"You're right, Brandon. I just don't even want to think about going back on Friday. I wish I had been expelled. Maybe it would be better for me to start over somewhere else."

Brandon laughed. "Oh yeah, like Dad would let you leave North Central!"

Even I had to laugh at that. Brandon had a way of lightening the mood, but I still knew that he cared about what was happening to me.

"Ya know, Leo, you already seem different—better. This is the first time we've really talked in a long while. I feel like I have my brother back." With that, he faked a punch to my nose and walked out of the room.

My mind analyzed the things that Brandon told me. I did feel better, but I knew Friday was going to be difficult. But at least Brandon was able to keep me aware of what they guys were saying, and what they knew.

I heard a little tap at my half-opened door, and my mom walked in my room. She held a tray in both hands. She set in on my nightstand.

"Dad said you hadn't eaten much, so I brought you a turkey sandwich and an iced tea."

She sat down beside me and placed her hand on my knee. "Bad day, huh."

"Kind of an understatement, Mom."

"Well, you look pretty crappy, so I'll let you eat. We can talk tomorrow. I just want you to know that I believe in you, Leo. You're one of the best people I know. We're all going to get through this. All your sadness is not going to disappear, but it will get better."

She kissed the top of my head and made a little sign of the cross on my forehead. "God bless you, Leo. Sleep well."

When she left, I was overwhelmed with gratitude for my whole family. I felt stupid that I had ever doubted that they understood me. Mrs. Franco, my parents, and Brandon, had all come through for me, and I started to realize that I did need other people. I could not get through this without trusting other people with the things I had buried deep inside me.

The sandwich and the iced tea disappeared quickly. I had not realized my hunger, and now I was extremely aware of how tired I felt. The sky had been dark for a while, and even though it was barely seven o'clock, my eyes felt heavy. I slipped under my covers and wrapped my arms around my extra pillow.

"Thank you, God, for opening my heart. Please help me with the things that I still need to face. Tell Jessie I love her." My heart still doubted that God would listen to me, but the prayer was a step to reconcile the terrible memories that I had to face. I was asleep within seconds.

Chapter 34

I FAINTLY REMEMBER HEARING my dad's car pull out of the driveway in the morning. Brandon usually left right after he did, but I must have fallen back to sleep. I was still struggling to wake up when my mom came into my room. She was ready to leave for work.

"Leo, don't sleep later than eight. You're not on vacation. A paper with your day's assignments is on the kitchen counter. Brandon will bring more assignments today, so get them done. I'll call on my break or at lunch, so please answer the phone. Love ya."

The door slammed a few minutes later, and I heard the garage door rolling shut. I fell back into a deep dream state of sleep. I was chasing butterflies in a beautiful green meadow. The faster I ran, the faster the butterflies flew away from me. When I looked down, I realized I wasn't wearing shoes. If I had remembered shoes, I thought, I probably could run faster. When I looked back up, the butterflies were gone, and the meadow had turned into a busy highway.

Those last thoughts startled me awake. My clock showed ten after eight; I'd had more than twelve hours of sleep.

By nine I was sitting in the family room with the television tuned to the Discovery Channel. My books and folders were on the coffee table in front of me. I grabbed the assignment folder from the kitchen counter and a coke from the fridge. I wasn't up to making myself breakfast, and I needed a shot of caffeine.

Mrs. Brunline's assignment paper was on the top. Along with some reading and questions from my literature book, some vocabulary sheets to study, and several grammar worksheets, there was an outline of a writing assignment. I carefully read through the directions for the writing exercise; Mrs. Brunline was a real stickler for following her every demand. She included a definition and some examples of an extended metaphor. She basically wanted us to write a poem using a lengthy metaphor with the same theme throughout.

My mind drew a blank, which was the case anytime I was under pressure to write. I reread the directions; nowhere did she state that rhyme was required. In the background the Discovery Channel was showing a picture of an erupting volcano. How could I compare Jessie to a volcano?

The words flowed quickly from my pen. Jessie was my muse, and I could make an analogy between her and any object. When I finished, I reread and did some slight modifications. I toyed with the idea of using Jessie's name as the title. I would have if the poem were for my eyes only. Instead, I titled it "The Impact of a Life."

You are a volcano
Your molten power spills onto the mountainside
Etching into the earth with its fiery mass
Erasing all the things in its path
Leaving behind a trail of steaming rock and ash.
And yet,
Destruction is not your goal.
Now that your essence is released
You unleash the potential for new life.
Emerging in weeks, in months, in years
A new beginning, a healthier, more vibrant growth
Than once was there.
How long will it take?
How long before I can begin again?

I was pleased with my work and even more pleased that it was something about Jessie. It was cryptic enough so that Mrs. Brunline would not connect it to a person who was mourning a lost love. The title disguised it as the importance of anyone's life.

I needed to type up my work, so I returned to my bedroom with my cola and rough draft in hand. I still could not look at or touch my computer without pining for a conversation with Jessie. I missed her more than words could ever express.

The poem read better now that it was typed, but the original had Jessie's name as the title. I opened the bottom drawer of my computer desk and pulled out the red and white striped Christmas bag that I kept tucked under some manila folders. I slid out the brown journal, my first gift from Jessie. My fingertips caressed the leather binding as I recalled the first touch of our hands on that cold winter afternoon almost two years ago.

Inside the still blank journal were copies of many of the poems that Jessie and I had written to one another. Some of them were handwritten on cards or papers, but most were copies of emails. My intention was to carefully print them into the blank journal, and then present it to Jessie on some important occasion.

I imagined her in a beautiful wedding gown. We would be in the back of a long, black limo after our huge church wedding. She would lean over to me, kiss me, and tell me that this was the happiest day of her life. I would smile and hand her this same red and white gift bag. Her eyes would glisten with tears when she opened the journal and saw the collection of our poetry.

That gift bag and journal had become the source of many more stories in my imagination. Every single story ended the same: Jessie would cry, kiss me passionately, and tell me she loved me.

Now the blank pages were just a reminder of how empty my life had become without her.

Chapter 35

MY MOTHER CALLED before noon to check on me. My report pleased her—my assignments were complete, and I intended to begin reading one of our assigned novels for this report period. She gave me a few more tasks to fill my day: shovel the light snow from the driveway, clean my room, take some laundry out of the dryer.

My stomach grumbled, so I toasted some frozen waffles and made a cup of hot chocolate. Every part of me wanted to turn on the television and get lost in a movie. I knew I was trying to avoid the assignment from Mrs. Franco.

Instead, I grabbed a jacket, ski hat, and gloves from our hallway closet. Then I went into our attached garage and rooted through a bin to find some boots. After I hit open the garage door, I found a snow shovel and cleaned the light coating of snow that covered our driveway and walkway.

Our neighborhood, including our house, was decorated with lights, reindeer, and other Christmas displays. Everything looked beautiful and perfect in the glistening, pristine snow. Christmas was one of my favorite times, but I dreaded it this year.

It was not the "season to be jolly" for me. Brandon was right—I didn't want to have a good time. It felt wrong to smile and laugh.

Mrs. Franco told me it was common for people who grieve to feel like that. We feel like we are not honoring the people who died when we feel joy, as if being happy would somehow hurt them or wrongly let others believe we had forgotten about the one we lost.

One time I had read about various grieving rituals of different people around the world. Some ancient people would gouge out an eye or tear out clumps of hair to show the pain they were feeling. Images of funeral processions in the Middle East flashed before my eyes; women were chanting and screaming loudly behind a coffin of a family member.

Now that I had experienced the death of someone I loved so dearly—someone I wanted to share my life with—I understood the need to be so public about feelings of grief. If I could tear out my hair and scream at the top of my lungs, maybe I would feel some release from my sadness. I felt that I didn't deserve to be happy.

For the moment, the physical exercise of shoveling snow and fighting the biting cold air gave me a little release. The wind cut into my skin, and my lips and fingertips were getting numb. The job was done for now, but probably by the time my mom arrived home, the falling snow would make it look like I hadn't done anything.

It was after two o'clock before I returned to my computer desk. My family would be home in a few hours, and I had not even started my writing for Mrs. Franco. I was truly a master of procrastination.

A blank document stared at me from my computer screen. I thought of the snow on the driveway. Would I do all of this work for nothing? Would the writing of my story ease my grief for a while, only to return and cover my life again?

Just begin, Leo. Write. Jessie deserves this. You need this.

Wednesday, August 16th, The Day That Jessie Died

It took me almost two hours to complete my writing to a point where I was somewhat satisfied. I heard some noises downstairs and knew my mother was home.

"Leo," she yelled up the steps, "I'm home. Come down so we can talk."

My mom had started dinner. Some pots were already on the stove, and she stood by the sink with a potato in her hand. She put it on the counter as soon as I entered the kitchen and sat at a stool on the kitchen island.

"Sit down with me, sweetie," she motioned towards an empty stool across from her.

After I sat down, she reached over for my hand. "Let me hear about your day, then I'll tell you about mine."

I gave her a description of my accomplishments but omitted the detail about the writing for Mrs. Franco. She seemed pleased that I had not wasted my day.

"Well, I talked with Mrs. Franco during my free period today. She said she wanted to alleviate some of my fears concerning you. I'm paraphrasing a little, but she thinks that the things that happened yesterday were a good turning point for you. That you are starting to open up and face . . ."

She stopped and seemed to be searching for words.

"Mom, it's okay. You can say Jessie's name. You can say that I'm learning to face Jessie's death."

She started to cry. Not a soft, small-tears-streaming-down-her-face cry, but a sobbing, shoulder shaking, hard-to-breathe cry. I walked over and stood behind her. My hand went to her hair, and as soon as I touched it, she stood up. We hugged, and she continued to sob into my shoulder.

"Oh, Leo, I miss her too," she whispered between sobs. "Our beautiful Jessie, your beautiful Jessie."

She eventually just sat down again and grabbed a napkin to dab away her tears.

"Leo, we were all blessed to have Jessie in our lives, even though that time wasn't long enough. She filled this house with her beautiful spirit the first day you brought her here. I'll never forget her. I don't want to forget her."

It was difficult for me to respond. I realized something then that had eluded me before. I wasn't the only person who'd lost Jessie. It really wasn't just my personal tragedy. Jessie's parents, her friends, my family . . . we all had a hole in our lives now.

"We'll help each other, Leo."

I smiled and walked to the sink. I picked up the potato peeler and a potato. "I could take over your kitchen duties and spend my prison time peeling potatoes. Of course, one potato might take me an hour to do. My skills in the kitchen aren't that great. "

Mom grabbed the peeler from my hand and pushed me aside with her hip.

"Go find something to do, Leo," she said. "The driveway could use another shoveling before your dad gets home."

"I love you, Mom," I said over my shoulder as I walked toward the garage.

Later my parents, Brandon, and I sat down to a dinner of potatoes and meatloaf. It was the first meal the four of us shared since Sunday. At first everyone seemed a little awkward and uncomfortable. It took Brandon to break the ice.

"You know, I never quite understood the reasoning behind suspensions. It seems to me that if you really want to punish a kid, you make them go to school longer, not give him a vacation."

He said it with such sincerity and seriousness, and I guess that's what I found funny. I started laughing, and soon we were all smiling.

"You're right, Brandon," my father countered, "it's like people being suspended with pay. What kind of punishment is that?"

"So," I said as I looked directly at Brandon, "you think I'm on vacation? Well, not only did Mom give me a long list of jobs to do, but I had assignments to do too. Don't think that's much of a vacation."

Brandon rolled his eyes. "Well, I hope the list Mom gives you for tomorrow allows you enough time to do today's school assignments. Wait till you see the folder of work I brought home from school for you. Old Mrs. Brunline's assignments alone will keep you busy most of the morning!"

In bed that night I thought about the occurrences of the last two days. Mrs. Franco was right. Since I had whacked Phil at school, things were changing for the best. Our discussion at dinner tonight was a good step. Our family actually shared some personal things instead of just talking about sports or the news.

The discussion with Mom made me look at the grief that others were feeling. Many other people shared my sorrow over Jessie's death. Specifically, my heart went to the Delaney family. I had not contacted them since the funeral. I lost my love, but they lost their only child. Maybe if I reached out to them, we could comfort each other.

But finally, the best transformation for me happened when I wrote my story for Mrs. Franco. I wasn't even concerned about Mrs. Franco's reaction to what I wrote. For some strange reason, when I put things on paper, it freed me from the torture of reliving those moments constantly in my head.

Chapter 36

MY LAST DAY OF SUSPENSION was definitely no vacation. I had started many of my assignments from school the night before, but it looked like I'd had hours of work to still complete. Mom went a little easy on me and only asked me to clean my room. She read through my folder of assignments, and she knew that I had a late afternoon appointment with Mrs. Franco.

That morning I made myself a good breakfast. Toast, scrambled eggs, and a big glass of orange juice got my day started. Everyone was already out of the house, and it was nearly eight by the time I finished eating.

I sat in front of the television in our family room while I sipped on my orange juice and completed some of my Algebra II homework. I'd finished my assignments from Mrs. Brunline last night. Her reading assignments took most of the evening. Now, after my math homework, I just had some social studies and science.

By noon every assignment from school was finished and placed in folders. I would give them to the respective teachers when I returned to classes tomorrow.

My meeting with Father Mike and Phil started to worry me, and I also was concerned about how my teachers and friends would respond to me. The last thing I wanted was to be the source of whispers in the hallways, or worse, to be treated differently. My months at North Central had been a good experience, and I didn't want anything to change.

I went to the kitchen and cleaned up the mess from breakfast. There were two slices of pizza in the fridge, so I microwaved them and carried them upstairs with me. I needed to print up my story for Mrs. Franco and get showered and ready. Dad was picking me up around three and taking me to my appointment.

I sat down at my desk and decided to play around on my computer before even opening my writing. I figured I deserved to take a relaxing lunch break after working so hard all morning. When I clicked open my email, I noticed mail from a source I didn't recognize.

It was an email from Mr. Delaney. I read it quickly first and then reread it several times.

Dear Leo,

Would you be able to meet with me this Saturday? I thought maybe you could come over around one o'clock. If that isn't possible, maybe you could give me some other time over the weekend that would work for you.

Dean Delaney

Mr. Delaney wanted to talk with me. It was both ominous and promising at the same time. We had an obvious bond in our love for Jessie, but I had never conversed with him in any real way. Now he wanted to meet with me. What did he want? More importantly, what could I handle talking about?

The email had been sent last night. More than likely he didn't know I was home from school today, and he wouldn't be home until later in the afternoon. That gave me some time to think about what I was going to do.

The pizza turned cold, and my appetite disappeared. I took my plate down to the kitchen and threw the pizza into the garbage. My mind swirled with thoughts. A talk with the Delaney's was another step to help me heal. Two questions plagued me: Was I ready to talk? How much was I ready to share?

By two o'clock the pages for Mrs. Franco were printed, and I was showered and ready for my appointment. The ride to the health clinic would take about a half hour. It would be an opportunity to discuss the email with my dad. Both he and Mrs. Franco needed to know about the correspondence.

During the hour wait for my dad, my avoidance techniques took over. Some cartoon shows gave my mind a rest from my worries.

Dad came home before three. He wanted to change and leave early for my appointment. He'd skipped lunch at work and wanted to stop for something to eat.

"Leo, would you like to eat at that diner close to North Central for lunch? I haven't been there in years, and they used to have the best burgers. What do ya say? Burgers, fries, and coke?"

We jumped in the car and headed toward the diner. Dad looked relaxed and comfortable since he changed to jeans and a golf shirt. He wore a suit and tie to work every day, but I knew his favorite outfit was any type of golf attire.

This December day was cold, but the sun was shining. We meandered our way through the downtown traffic and listened to some sports talk on the radio. Dad said very little except to comment on the sports analysis.

We found a parking space right in front of the diner. The diner wasn't crowded since it was after lunch and before dinner, so we sat right down at a booth by the window. A waitress took our order of burgers, fries, and cokes.

"So, Leo, did you manage to get all your work done? I saw the folder of assignments that Brandon brought home, so I know you had a lot to do."

"Well, I actually got a head start last night, so I finished by lunch."

"I guess that gave you plenty of time to think about your session with Mrs. Franco. I know she's going to talk about your meeting with Phil and Father Mike tomorrow. I hope you're not too worried about going back to school."

"I'm a little nervous. But Dad, there's actually something else that has me worried."

My dad listened and nodded his head as I told him about the email from Mr. Delaney. He looked concerned, and he didn't say anything right away. He stared out the window for a moment.

"I don't know what to tell you, Leo. I've never really talked to Mr. Delaney much either. The only real time I spent with him was the few evenings at the funeral parlor. He didn't say much, but he told me that I should be proud of you. He said that Jessie spoke of you often, and that he knew . . . well, he knew that you and Jessie loved each other."

"I just don't know what he might want to talk to me about, Dad. I'm just nervous about the whole thing. Honestly, the guy kinda scares me."

My dad laughed. "I know what you mean. But, Leo, he's a good guy. I know some people who have dealt with him in his business. They all said the same thing. He's an honest, respectable man who works hard. I think maybe he just needs to talk to somebody who loved Jessie as much as he did."

"So you think I should go?"

"I wouldn't force you to do anything you're uncomfortable with, Leo. But, yes, I think it would be good for you. You need to talk about Jessie, and he needs to do that too. I know when your grandpap died, I didn't accept his death until I talked about how he had lived. His death was very hard on me, and I didn't even want to look at a picture of him for the longest time. Your Grandma Lily was the one who made me realize that talking about him was good for all of us. She said that all our memories helped keep him with her."

"I guess it wouldn't hurt to see what he wants."

"Think about it for a while. You could always postpone the meeting to another time."

We ended our lunch with apple pie, and we were stuffed. Dad took the time to text Mom that she should not worry about dinner. We would pick up something for her and Brandon on the way home.

When we got to the health clinic, Dad decided to wait inside with me. We both sat in the waiting room until Mrs. Franco came out to greet us.

"Nice to see you, Mr. Harrison. If you need some coffee or a donut while you wait, I have some in my office. I can bring it out to you before we get started."

Dad patted his stomach. "No thanks, Mrs. Franco, Leo and I just got done eating. I think we're both fine for the rest of the day."

"Okay, then. Read some magazines or take a nap. Lee will be done in about forty minutes."

Once we were in Mrs. Franco's office, we took our usual seats across from each other. I placed a folder with a copy of my story on the table between us.

"I finished writing everything down for you, Mrs. Franco."

"Good, Lee. I don't know if that's the reason, but there's an obvious difference in you. This is the first session we've had together where there is a smile in your eyes and a more relaxed tone in your voice."

"I do feel better, Mrs. Franco. For the first time since August, I'm starting to feel like . . . I can't really describe it . . . but, I feel like I'm back in my own skin. For all these months it was almost like I was in a bubble and just watched the world go by."

"You know, Lee, from what you told me about Jessie, she would want you to live your life to the fullest."

Mrs. Franco was right. Jessie made her short life so important to many people. I needed to make her proud of me again.

We talked about my meeting tomorrow morning at school. She offered to be there as support for me, but I told her it wasn't necessary. If things were going to change, I needed to speak for myself and handle my problems.

When we finished talking about the meeting, I told Mrs. Franco about Mr. Delaney's request to talk with me.

"The timing seems wrong, Lee. You've had a difficult week, and you still have your meeting at school tomorrow. It might be too much for you. Is there a way you could postpone it?"

"I haven't answered his email yet, so I could say that it would be best to schedule our talk for another time."

"It is a good idea to talk to him at some point. That's another hurdle you have to jump. You can't avoid the Delaney's forever. I think you have to weigh the pros and cons of meeting him at this moment. You can decide when you think the best time might be."

Mrs. Franco picked up the folder from the table. "I think I'll read this later if you don't mind. We'll have another session next week, and I'll have time to read this carefully before then."

"Mrs. Franco," the anxiety in my voice was apparent even to me, "I don't exactly know what to expect from you after you read it. But, well, . . . I guess I just want you to know that I'm glad you asked me to write it. No matter what, things do feel better now. Even things with my family have been different. "

"Grief is a difficult thing, Lee. But, I think you've discovered that it's not going to go away just because you don't talk about it."

Dad was in the reception area, sitting in a corner chair with his long legs stretched straight out in front of him. His arms were crossed at his chest, and his eyes were closed. As I looked at him, I realized how difficult all my problems were for him and my mother. They were both probably as physically and emotionally exhausted as I was.

Dad sensed my presence and opened his eyes. "Everything okay, Leo?"

"Yep," I smiled, "we're good to go, Dad."

As promised, we picked up some take-out chicken for Mom and Brandon. My mom was in the kitchen when we arrived home. She got drinks and plates out for her and Brandon. After we said hello, Dad put the take-out bag on the counter and opened the containers of chicken and mashed potatoes.

Instead of disappearing to my room like I normally would have, I sat down at the kitchen island. My mom turned when she heard the stool scratch along the ceramic tile. She smiled, obviously happy that I stuck around.

"Would you like some, Leo? Your dad ordered enough for a football team, so I think you could have a piece or two."

"No thanks, Mom, we had a pretty big lunch. The burgers at the diner were huge, and the apple pie was almost as good as Gram's."

Dad yelled upstairs to Brandon to let him know dinner had arrived. He sat down beside me, and Mom joined us too.

"Anything you want to share?" Mom asked.

"It was a good day, Mom. I just want you and Dad to know that . . . well, to know how much I appreciate everything. I know this hasn't been easy on you either."

"Leo, we would do anything for you. We're a family, and what hurts you, hurts us. But, we wouldn't have it any other way."

She got up and came around me from behind. Her arms wrapped around my shoulders, and she kissed me on the back of my head. Dad reached over and squeezed my hand.

Just then, Brandon walked in the room. "I guess I missed another Hallmark moment at the Harrison's," he said with a wry smile. "I don't care, as long as there's still some chicken left."

Mom let go of me and walked over to Brandon. She hugged him and kissed his cheek. "Don't worry Brandon, there's enough chicken and love to go around."

Later that evening we all watched some television together. It was nice just to relax with the whole family. *Frosty the Snowman*, a favorite Christmas cartoon, began at eight o'clock. Brandon and I took turns annoying Mom and Dad by reciting some of the parts.

After nine, we all confessed to being tired. While Mom and Dad turned out lights and secured doors, Brandon and I headed up to bed.

"It's going to be okay tomorrow, Leo. Guys forget about things quickly and move on. The fight you had with Phil is old news now. Most of the guys are too busy talking about the rumor that old man Sweeney is going to get fired."

Sweeney was North Central's Spanish teacher and basketball coach. He had coached our team for over a decade. Now, not only was our basketball team having one of its worst seasons ever, but Mr. Sweeney had gotten into a big argument with a parent of an opposing team at a recent game. He had screamed, yelled some profanities, and made some threatening motions to the parent. Poor sportsmanship from any of our players was never tolerated, and it certainly would not be accepted by a coach who represented our school. According to Brandon, the big topic of discussion was who would replace Sweeney. A new basketball coach was the focus of everyone's gossip since the game on Wednesday night.

"Thanks, Brandon. You're probably right. Nothing takes center stage like a teacher making a fool of himself and getting fired."

I went straight to my computer when I got to my room. I needed to respond to Mr. Delaney's email, and Mrs. Franco and my dad both indicated that postponing it might be the best option. When I reread it though, I was struck by a feeling of urgency. Mr. Delaney wrote that he wanted to meet Saturday or "some other time over the weekend." I thought about how much better I felt since I talked about my feelings. Why not just meet with him and get it over with? I would just worry and be anxious until I discovered what he wanted. So, I sent an email that said I would meet him at one on Saturday.

As I sat at my desk, I said a little prayer. "Lord, I don't deserve your forgiveness. But I need strength to get through the next few weeks."

Chapter 37

Dad drove me to school the next morning. My meeting with Father Mike and Phil was at seven, and the bus wouldn't get me there on time. My dad walked me into the school and talked to Miss Whiley. He had papers to sign, and at least one parent had to be present when a student returned to school from a suspension. Miss Whiley told me to go to Father Mike's office. Phil had not yet arrived.

Before I walked away, my dad put his hand on my shoulder. "You'll be okay, Leo."

There was a tone in his voice that made me confident that he was right. I nodded my thanks to him and walked slowly to Father Mike's office.

Father's office door was slightly open, and I could see him at his desk. He waved me in.

"Have a seat, Lee. Phil isn't here yet, so we have some time to talk."

He closed the door and then sat in a chair beside me.

Father Mike was probably only in his mid-thirties. He was tall and thin and had a boyish look that sometimes caused him to be mistaken for a student. He was known around campus as a good guy. His door was always open to anyone who had a problem, and he had a reputation for being a good listener.

"So, Lee, you've put in your suspension time. Are you ready to get back to the school routine again?"

"I think so, Father," I answered in a tone that was much more confident than I actually felt. "I just wish I could get this day over with."

"Lee, mostly everyone, including myself, knows the reason you lost your temper on Tuesday. That's one of the reasons I'm glad we have a little time before Phil gets here. I know you're seeing a grief counselor, but I want you to know that I'd like to help you too, if I can."

I nodded in agreement. But, as sincere as Father Mike sounded, I doubted very much if he could relate to my feelings. What would he, a priest, understand about my love for Jessie?

As if he read my thoughts, Father Mike said, "I know you think that, given my vocation as a priest, I might not be able to relate to your feelings, Lee. But, I was young once too. I had a few romantic relationships when I was young. But, that's really not the common ground we share."

He paused and ran his fingers through his sandy colored hair. Whatever the common ground was, he seemed reluctant to share it with me. He stood and walked to his office window. When he spoke, it hardly seemed as if he was talking to me.

"When I was a junior in high school, I lost someone very close to me. My younger sister. She was only fifteen when she died. We grew up in a pretty rural area in Ohio. There wasn't another house within five miles of our family home. She and I were close in age, and we grew up as best friends."

When he turned back towards me, the sadness of his memory showed on his whole body. His shoulders slumped, and his eyes were somewhat blank and lifeless. I wondered if this was the way I looked to others since Jessie died.

"Father, if you don't mind telling me, how did she die?"

"People find it hard to believe, mostly because of the type of lifestyle our family had, but Sarah died of alcohol poisoning. We were a good, loving, God-fearing family who lived in the sticks. But, it took only one stupid party at a friend's house, and one bad decision by Sarah, and her beautiful life ended."

"Do you ever stop thinking about that? What I mean is . . . do you ever stop wondering about what she missed because she died so young . . . or what you missed not having her grow up with you?"

"This might not be the answer that you want to hear, Lee. But, I want to be honest with you. There have been very few days since her death that I've not thought about her. At first I felt a lot of anger with myself. You know, if onlys . . . if only I had been at that party, if only I had stopped her from going, if only I had been a better older brother. Now, I'm more in the "I wish" stage. I wish I could tell her about what I did today. I wish I could share that great book with her. And yes, I wish I could have officiated at her wedding or baptized her children."

I expected the "she's in a better place" speech from someone who was a priest. Instead, he spoke of the type of loss that I understood perfectly.

We both heard the approaching footsteps at the same time. Father looked up at the clock and shook his head in disgust.

"That must be Phil. I'm sorry, Lee. Let me tell him to wait. This meeting wasn't supposed to be about my problems."

"Father, it's fine. What you said . . . about your sister . . . well, it kinda made me feel like you do understand."

"Thanks, Lee," he said as his hand went to my shoulder, "I do want you to know that you can come and talk anytime. We can help each other."

There was a tap at the door. Father gave me a smile that conveyed his confidence in my ability to get through this little hurdle. After all, he understood the bigger things that I already overcame.

Our meeting lasted less than thirty minutes. Father Mike made sure we understood how we were both at fault. Phil was insensitive and totally out of line when he ridiculed something that he had no right to read, and I was wrong in dealing with the issue with violence. Phil and I just nodded in agreement, and then Father asked us to face each other and apologize.

I went first. "Phil, I really didn't mean to hit you. I honestly was so angry and upset that I don't remember much. It was just that I wanted that poem back. I'm sorry."

"Sure, Lee. I was really being a jerk with what I did. I didn't know . . . you know . . . I didn't understand how much that poem meant to you. I wasn't thinking . . . I'm so sorry . . . you know, for everything."

We shook hands. Phil had a hard time looking at me. It was apparent that he knew about Jessie now, and he obviously felt bad about teasing me.

Father reminded us of the consequences of any further problems, and then he sent us to our homeroom. Phil grabbed his backpack from outside Father's office door and darted down the hall. He still didn't seem to want to be near me. I quickened my pace to catch up with him.

"Hey, Phil," I said when I managed to get beside him, "what's the latest on Coach Sweeney? I hear he's going to be out of a job soon."

Phil slowed down and took a little breath. "Yeah, man, wait until you meet the crazy-ass sub they hired to take his place. I hope they don't decide to hire him permanently."

By the time we got to homeroom, we talked like good buddies. The few kids who were already in class seemed surprised that we looked so chummy. Mr. Simmons looked up from his desk and motioned for us to get settled. There was a hint of a smile on his face.

"Glad to see you two have mended your fences," he said. "But, there are only fifteen minutes till morning bell, so get yourselves ready."

The rest of the day went fairly smoothly. I mentally thanked Brandon for telling me about Mr. Sweeney. It became my deflection for anyone who wanted to ask me too many questions or just got too personal in their comments to me. I accepted the "I'm really sorry about your girlfriend" comments with a nod and "Thanks, man" response. But, I used the Sweeney card anytime a guy pressed for details about what had happened to her.

When I stepped off the bus after school that day, I felt proud of how the day had gone. A point for you, Leo, I thought. I'd face a separate battle tomorrow when I met with Mr. Delaney. But, right now, I wanted to reward myself for a job well done and distract myself from the challenge ahead.

Jordan answered his cell right away. He, of course, was surprised that I called him.

"Hey, Jordan, what ya been up to?" I felt somewhat nervous about the call. It had been more than a month since I talked to him.

"Nothin' much, what about you?" His tone didn't reveal anything.

"Want to take in a movie tonight? There are lots of new releases, and at least two I'd like to see."

"Oh, that's gonna be tough, Leo. I had plans. There are three hot senior chicks who were planning on spending time with me tonight. But, well, for you man, I guess I could reschedule."

Jordan was the embodiment of true friendship. He welcomed me back, no questions asked. We planned to leave around seven that night. I knew Mom or Dad could drive us, and Jordan was sure his dad wouldn't mind picking us up at eleven. We would decide on the movie after we got to the cinema at the mall. Whatever time before or after the movie, we could spend eating, shopping, or just looking at Christmas displays.

The movie was action packed and entertaining, and Jordan and I spent our time catching up. I didn't tell him about my suspension; we were having too good a time for me to share anything that might make the mood serious. The only somewhat serious comment I made was when Jordan's dad dropped me off at home.

"Thanks, Jordan," I said as I punched him in the shoulder. "It's always great to spend time with you. Let's do something over Christmas vacation, okay?"

"I'll clear my calendar, bro. See ya soon."

Chapter 38

I AWOKE EARLY the next morning. My body was filled with a nervous energy because of my impending meeting with Mr. Delaney. No one else was awake, so I decided to get dressed and shovel the driveway. A light snow had fallen overnight, and the exercise of shoveling was exactly what I needed. By the time I finished, Mom and Dad were up and making breakfast. We sat down to some French toast and sausage. Surprisingly, Brandon slept through the aromas that filled the house.

"Leo, Dad told me about your meeting with Mr. Delaney this afternoon. Is there anything you need from us? Maybe Dad or I could just call him and get a feel for what he wants."

"I'm fine, Mom. I should have talked to him way before this. It's just that . . . well, you know, I wasn't quite ready. He really deserves to talk to me. It's the least I can do."

At almost exactly one o'clock, I knocked on the Delaney's front door. Mrs. Delaney's car was not in the driveway, so she was probably at work. It would just be the two of us. I touched the folded papers in my jacket pocket and wondered how much courage I would have today.

Mr. Delaney opened the door. He motioned me into the foyer.

"Take off your jacket, Leo, just throw it on the bench there and come on in. I thought maybe you'd like to sit with me in the kitchen. I made us both a cup of hot chocolate."

We entered the Delaney's spacious kitchen. I noticed very few Christmas decorations aside from the snowman placemats and a snowman dish filled with assorted cookies. I sat down on one of the four chairs around the oak kitchen table, and Mr. Delaney brought over two big mugs of hot chocolate and sat beside me.

"I took the liberty of fixing you my special hot cocoa, Leo. A dash of cinnamon and a big squirt of whipped cream."

"Smells delicious, sir," I said as I wrapped my hands around the warm mug.

"Leo, if you don't mind, just call me Dean. 'Mr. Delaney' makes me feel old, and 'sir' makes me feel like you should salute, too."

I laughed nervously. Mr. Delaney was trying his best to make me feel comfortable, but it wasn't quite working.

"Leo, it took me this long to work up the courage to talk to you. I feel so lost without Jessie. She was . . . well . . . I guess you could say, she was my soul, my conscience. Sometimes in the middle of the night I swear I hear her say, 'Dad, you gotta talk to Leo.'"

"I miss her, too," I said as I looked into the melting swirl of cream in my mug.

"I know, Leo. She never said it outright, but I knew she loved you. The two of you had something very special."

The surprised and embarrassed expression on my face actually made Mr. Delaney smile.

"Let me ease your concerns, Leo. I only want to talk about some things that Jessie might have left unsaid."

"Unsaid?"

Mr. Delaney took a big, long sigh, and then he paused as if to gather his thoughts.

"I'm really making a mess of this, son. I guess I have to start somewhere that probably won't make any sense to you. But it is something you need to know to understand the whole story."

So, over a cup of hot chocolate, Mr. Delaney began his story. He stopped every once in a while to munch on a cookie and sip his cocoa.

Dean Delaney had grown up in Erie, Pennsylvania, which is only about two hours north of Pittsburgh. He and a younger brother, Mark, were raised by their mom. His father died of a heart attack when Mr. Delaney was only three and his brother had just turned two. Respect and admiration came through in his voice as he told the story of how his mom took on the difficult task of raising two young children on her own.

"We were poor in everything but love, Leo. Mom raised Mark and me to watch out for each other. So, when she died a few months after I turned twenty-one, I knew it was my job to watch over my little brother."

Mr. Delaney worked for a construction company in Erie then. He tried to talk his brother into going to college, but Mark refused. The two ended up working for the same company. They purchased a big, old house and worked on remodeling it on the weekends. The only time they weren't building or rebuilding something was on Saturday night.

"Me and Mark would get all cleaned up and go to the local bar early on Saturday evenings. We would order a big steak dinner and drink beer until midnight. But it wasn't really the food or the drinks that brought us back to that bar each week."

Mr. Delaney said that he and Mark both were infatuated with a beautiful, young waitress named Jessica. Even though she was only eighteen, she was already on her own. She lived with a roommate who'd had a similar background. Both were raised by parents who had issues with drugs and alcohol and were abusive. The girls met as teens, and as soon as they graduated from high school, they decided to leave home and make a life for themselves.

"Everyone came to that dive of a bar to see Jessica. She was young, gorgeous, and could always make you smile, no matter how bad your week had been."

I could see Mr. Delaney's face light up with the memory of her. I wondered if Mrs. Delaney knew this story.

"Mark was young and handsome and had a personality that made everyone love him. So, even though she had many suitors, Jessica fell hard for my little brother."

Mark and Jessica became inseparable, and before long Jessica got pregnant. Mr. Delaney said that instead of being upset, both of them were excited about having a child.

"They were so much in love that they really weren't thinking about all the consequences. Mark and I argued a lot then. I finally agreed to let Jessica move in with us. We had plenty of space in the big, old house, so Jessica asked if her roommate could move in, too. It all made sense since it would save everyone money in the long run."

So, Dean and Mark Delaney, Jessica, and her roommate, Sharon, made a home for themselves. Jessica quit working a month before the baby was born. Mr. Delaney said it was one of the happiest times of his life. They became a little family, something that each one of them needed.

"Jessica was so excited about the baby, and the rest of us prepared the baby's room and even started to make plans for the wedding. Jessica wanted to wait until the baby was two months old to give herself time to slim down for her wedding."

I was so engrossed in the story that it took me a while to connect all the dots. But, I began to get some sense of where the story was headed when I realized that the roommate, Sharon, was Mrs. Delaney.

Mr. Delaney's eyes filled with tears when he recalled the birth of the new baby.

"I can remember almost every moment of that day. Jessica and Mark sitting on the living room floor and laughing as they kept track of her contractions. Me and Sharon running around making sure we had everything for the hospital. And then, all of us piling into Mark's car and making the trip to the hospital. We were all so close that it was hard to tell who was the most excited."

Chapter 39

WHEN MR. DELANEY continued the story at that point, he looked right into my eyes. He could see me adding up the clues, and he smiled.

"Yep, Leo," he said with a voice that displayed love and pride, "we welcomed a beautiful baby girl into our lives about five hours after we got to the hospital. We were all there at the birth. I was the third person to hold her. Mark said something about how he now had a 'little Jessica' to love. Then he said, 'Jessie—I think we'll call her Jessie.' They had never even mentioned that as one of the names they were considering, but all of us nodded in agreement. It seemed like a perfect choice."

"So, Jessie was really your niece and not your daughter?" At this point my mind was exploding with questions, and I sat straight up in my chair. Mr. Delaney gestured with his hand in a calming fashion.

"I know you probably have lots of questions, Leo. But let me finish the whole story. There are some things I want to make sure you understand."

My body slid back into the chair, and I waited for Mr. Delaney to continue. This part of the story had to be the hardest for him to tell.

"We brought Jessie home from the hospital, and we all became a doting, loving family. Jessie was so spoiled.

I don't think she actually used her crib for the first few weeks she was home. We just kept passing her around. Nobody wanted to lay her down."

Mr. Delaney described the joy that Jessie brought to their home. They decided that Jessica should not go back to work. Her job would be to take care of the house and, of course, take care of Jessie.

Almost four months after Jessie was born, Mark and Jessica finally decided to get married.

"We planned a small wedding and reception at the house. All our remodeling was finished, and we were ready to show the place off. Sharon added her special touch by planting flowers and preparing a place in the yard for the ceremony."

Mr. Delaney stopped. He got up and stood at the kitchen counter. He rinsed his mug and then filled it with some tap water.

"The whole day was perfect. Everyone enjoyed themselves and made a big fuss over sweet little Jessie."

He took a sip of water and sat back down. His voice was getting tired, but we were both anxious to get to the end of the story.

"Later that night, after the last guests left, I told Jessica and Mark that I had a surprise for them. As my wedding gift, I had booked them on a short honeymoon vacation. It was nothing elaborate, but it was the best I could afford. I had made arrangements for them to stay at a hotel right on the bay of Lake Erie for a four-day weekend getaway. Their meals, the room, and even a twilight cruise were all paid for."

As Mr. Delaney continued his narration, I pictured everything in my head. Since I had never seen Jessie's birth parents, I imagined an older version of me and Jessie in the story.

"Jessica started to cry when I told her about my gift. She had never been on any kind of vacation, and I guess all the events of the day had just overwhelmed her. I remember Sharon hugging Jessica and telling her that everything would be fine. We promised we would take good care of baby Jessie while they were away."

My heart beat painfully in my chest. I knew there was no happily-ever-after ending coming. Jessie obviously had not grown up with her real parents.

"They left for the trip a few weeks after the wedding. They were only going to be half an hour away on the shores of Lake Erie, but they couldn't contain their excitement. They left on a Friday morning, bright and early. Jessica and Mark each held Jessie for the longest time. Jessica handed Jessie to me. She said, 'Here, Uncle Dean, take care of my little sweetheart. Make sure you tell her every day how much I love her and miss her.' Those were the last words she ever said to me."

Mr. Delaney stopped more and more during his story. He tried to keep his composure. He stood up often and turned away to take a sip of water. After a while, he would sit down and continue for a few more sentences. Because I needed so badly to hear the rest of this story, I endured his torture without saying anything.

"Mark and Jessica spent that first day enjoying the beach, eating a great dinner, and staying at the hotel on the bay. Jessica called and talked to Sharon the next morning. She told Sharon that she and Mark were having breakfast at the hotel, and then planned on exploring the shops. They were scheduled for the twilight dinner cruise at six and would probably get back to the hotel after eleven. She wanted to call then, if it wasn't too late.

"We didn't hear from her that night and figured they had gotten back too late. We woke up early that Sunday morning. Sharon and I wanted to do something special with Jessie, maybe go to the park or for a stroll at the mall. We heard a car pull up outside. As soon as I saw that it was a Pennsylvania State trooper, I knew bad news was coming."

The twilight cruise that Mr. Delaney booked was involved in an accident in the middle of Lake Erie. It was only a small ship with the capacity of about one hundred people. A thirty-foot sailboat hit into its side during the cruise. Most of the people had been rescued, but seven people, who were on the deck where the sailboat hit, were killed. Jessie's parents were two of those people.

"Two beautiful lives cut short, and Jessie was left to grow up without them. You know, Leo, it took me years to get over the guilt I felt about sending them on that trip. Very few days go by when I don't think of the way things could have been."

At this point, Mr. Delaney was not even hiding his tears. He just wiped them with the back of his flannel shirt cuff. His eyes had the same green shine that had made Jessie's eyes so beautiful. My instinct was to just remain quiet. I feared that he might become so emotional that he wouldn't be able to continue.

"It took weeks for all the complications from the accident to settle. We needed to meet with lawyers and settle with the company who owned the sailboat. Then we had to worry about Jessie. There was no will, and I had to prove that I was willing and capable to care for her. I was Mark's only living relative, but Jessica's family had to be contacted too. Sharon and I could never have given her up. We worried every day that someone would come and try to take her from us. For quite some time we had been attracted to one another, but never really had a romantic relationship. It was Sharon who suggested we get married because it would make an adoption easier. We did a quick civil ceremony, and within a month after the accident, I was a married man with a baby daughter."

That memory made him smile. I was touched by his obvious love for Jessie and for Mrs. Delaney.

"We stayed in Erie for almost two years after the accident. Then I had a job offer in the Pittsburgh area, and, after a great deal of thought, I decided to move our family here. We rented a little apartment and had some happy years there. When Jessie was five, we bought this house. It reminded us so much of the place we had in Erie. We wanted to raise Jessie in a good, loving home and give her all the things that Sharon and I didn't have in our childhood."

"You did, Mr. Delaney," I said with complete sincerity. "Jessie was proud of her family, and I know how much she loved you."

"Thank you, Leo," he said as he played with the cookie dish in the middle of the table. "But I have so much guilt over so many things. It wasn't just the guilt over sending them on that trip. It was so much more than that. Jessica's last request to me was to remind Jessie every day how much her mother loved her and missed her. And, I broke that promise."

My cell rang and startled us both. Mr. Delaney motioned to me to answer it, and then he walked into the living room. I wasn't sure if he wanted to give me privacy, or if he just needed to take a break.

"Leo," my dad asked, "is everything okay? Are you still at the Delaney's?"

"I'm fine, Dad. Me and Mr. Delaney are still talking. I'll walk home when we're done."

"Okay. I just didn't expect you to be very long. Call me if you need anything."

After I put my cell away, I sat for several minutes before Mr. Delaney returned. He held some photos in his hand.

"These are some pictures of Jessie, mostly from the last few years. I thought maybe you would like them. I have other copies."

"Thanks, Mr. Delaney, I only have a few school pictures and some candids on my phone. I really appreciate it."

As I looked through the pictures, my heart ached for Jessie.

"Did she know . . . about the accident, about . . ." I was having a hard time posing the right question to Mr. Delaney. I wanted him to continue where he left off.

"Well, that's the part I really need to tell you. It might explain some things to you."

"After Sharon and I married, we became so much of a real family. We referred to each other as 'Mom' and 'Dad' when we talked to Jessie. I kept telling myself that I would tell her about her real parents when she got older. At first, my excuse was that she was too young to understand. Then . . . well, then I just thought it was too late and there was no reason she really needed to know. After all, she and I were flesh and blood. We looked enough alike that people knew she belonged to me. What good would come of her knowing anyone but me as her father?"

It was true. People often commented about those pale green eyes that they both had. Jessie also had Mr. Delaney's smile and a similar gait when she walked. No one would have questioned that they were father and daughter.

"But in the sixth grade Jessie started asking Sharon questions about her pregnancy and Jessie's birth. Sharon kept the answers general enough that she never really lied to Jessie. But, she told me we had to tell Jessie the truth. The questions were getting more difficult for Sharon to answer, and I was haunted by Jessica's last words to me. So, at the end of Jessie's seventh grade school year, we decided to tell Jessie everything. We planned a trip to Erie. We wanted to show Jessie where we all had lived, and take her to Mark and Jessica's grave site. We even rehearsed what we would say."

I remembered that summer well. I thought of Jessie's poem about us being two ships passing in the night. Did Mr. Delaney know that Jessie and I were close then?

"It was a difficult weekend for all of us that June. Jessie did not say much when we told her the things that had happened to her real parents. She asked some questions when we took her to the house and the grave site, and she also wanted to see the hotel where Mark and Jessica had spent their last night. I had to leave for Pittsburgh on Sunday because I had to work the next day. Jessie could barely look me in the eye when I said goodbye. She was hurt and angry. I thought I had lost her forever. Sharon called me every day from Erie, but not once did Jessie ask to talk to me. Sharon was concerned but kept reassuring me that it was a lot for Jessie to absorb. We had to let her process what we told her."

"Sharon and Jessie spent the next few weeks together at a cabin along Lake Erie. I was there only on the weekends. Jessie seemed to get angrier with every day that passed. The only thing she would say to me was that I should have told her. When those few weeks were up, Sharon wasn't sure if it was a good idea for Jessie to stay in Erie for the two-week camp she had signed up for. But Jessie said she needed the time away from us to think about everything."

I would have been hurt and angry too. Jessie probably felt like most of her life was a lie.

"I called the camp every day to check on her, but she would never talk to me. One time she called and spoke to Sharon on her first weekend away, but only to tell her that she would rather not have us call anymore. She just gave us the time to pick her up the following week. Sharon went by herself to get her and bring her home. Most of that summer she avoided talking to us, and she spent a lot of time in her room or out with some of her friends. She didn't call us 'Mom' or 'Dad' anymore and wouldn't even sit down to dinner with us. Sharon cried every night. It was so hard on both of us, but I felt more like I deserved it."

Mr. Delaney's voice started to sound strained. He had probably never talked so long in his life. He sipped some more water and asked me if I wanted more hot chocolate or something cold to drink. I just nodded my decline.

"Jessie started asking Sharon some more specific questions like: What was the name of the hospital where she was born? What was her mother's maiden name? Where had Jessica been born? Sharon said that she was doing research online, trying to discover more information about her mother. Sharon was as patient and understanding as anyone could possibly be, but eventually she just couldn't take it anymore. One day Sharon stomped into Jessie's room where Jessie was sitting at her computer. She told Jessie that, if she wanted to know anything about her real mom, she should ask one of us. After all, we were all best friends and had shared everything the last few years of Mark and Jessica's life."

It was hard for me to picture Mrs. Delaney getting angry, but I was slowly learning that there were more sides to the Delaney family than I had ever imagined.

"Jessie slowly started talking to us again. By the time she started school that year, she was at least talking more to Sharon. She still was shutting me out though, and it was killing me to see the pain in her eyes."

I didn't need to be reminded of the pain in Jessie's eyes or the change in her personality that summer. All those months, when I believed that she no longer cared about me, she was dealing with the pain and anger of Mr. Delaney's deception. So many things started to make sense to me.

"It wasn't until right before Thanksgiving that our relationship improved. Her attitude toward me had softened and that veil of sadness was slowly lifting from her eyes. The Saturday before Thanksgiving I awoke in the middle of the night and couldn't sleep. I came down here to the kitchen and fixed myself some tea. I didn't even turn on any lights . . . there was plenty of reflected light from outside. I sat right here, sipping my tea and thinking about how I had screwed up my relationship with Jessie. I heard footsteps, but I figured it was Sharon. I looked up and Jessie was standing over by that doorway. All she said was 'Dad,' the word I had been waiting to hear for months. I jumped out of my chair and ran to her. We hugged and cried. I just kept saying, 'I'm so sorry, Jessie, so sorry.' After that, we talked. Not really long—just long enough for her to say that she was more confused than angry. She knew I loved her, but I was wrong to hide so much from her."

Mr. Delaney stood up again and ran his fingers through his hair. He was emotionally exhausted from revisiting such serious memories. My feelings about Mr. Delaney ran from sympathy to anger, and I wasn't sure if I should tell him that. But, all of me understood that he never meant to hurt Jessie.

"Mr. Delaney, Jessie obviously forgave you and learned to accept the truth about your relationship. It might have been hard for her at first, but there's no doubt in my mind that she understood how difficult the whole situation was for you."

"Did she ever say anything to you, Leo . . . about my not being her father or about any of this?"

"No, sir, she didn't," I said as my mind did a fast replay of our summer breakup.

Mr. Delaney gave a short laugh. "I guess you're never going to call me Dean."

I smiled at him. And, for the first time since we started, I made eye contact with him. If there was anyone who understood Mr. Delaney's feelings of guilt and sadness, I was that person.

"Jessie was the best person I ever knew. You and Mrs. Delaney raised her to be that way."

"Thanks, Leo. It means a lot to me that you said that. Life without Jessie has been so difficult for me and Sharon. I guess I just need to deal with my loss by remembering I did all I could to make her happy while she was alive. I just screwed up so much with the choices I made years ago. But, Leo, I want you to know that it gives me a lot of comfort knowing that Jessie got to experience a loving relationship like you two had. You made her happy."

"We both made her happy, Mr. Delaney. And we all made some bad choices. You made things right with Jessie, and I guess that's what really matters."

I rose and pushed my chair under the table. There was so much for me to think about, and not much more I wanted to say. Mr. Delaney had confessed his sins to me, and it was obvious that he felt some relief.

"I'd better get home, Mr. Delaney."

He walked me to the door, where I picked up my jacket from the bench in the entranceway. I felt the stiffness of the papers in my jacket pocket. After the long afternoon with Mr. Delaney, I felt a bond with him. But this moment didn't seem right. Mr. Delaney was emotionally fatigued. The narrative about the day Jessie died could wait for another time.

These secret words I hold so near
They beg to find a listening ear.
But somehow words don't seem to flow
Before my courage starts to go.
If I could share what's in my heart
Away the foolish thoughts would dart.
For secret words weigh on my soul
My every thought they do control.

If only they would disappear,
Instead they whisper in my ear.
Reminding me of my own fear.
These secret words, these secret words.

Chapter 40

I RETURNED HOME and found everyone anxious to hear about my meeting with Mr. Delaney. By the time Sunday dinner was on the table, everyone in the family, including Grandma Lily, knew the story of Jessie's true relationship to Dean and Sharon Delaney. I hadn't asked Mr. Delaney's permission to share his story, so I emphasized that it should just remain among us.

Mom seemed the most floored by the revelation, but she was sympathetic to the whole situation.

"He's had so much tragedy in his life. Now he and Sharon have no one. I just can't imagine all the things they've been through."

Gram nodded her head in agreement. "They've lost so much of their family, and yet neither one of them ever appears bitter or angry. When I think about how Sharon reached out to the women at the shelter, I'm even more impressed."

Gram's comment made me think back to how excited Jessie was with her volunteer work. After last Christmas, she talked so much about her plans to help the young mothers and their children.

Jessie and Mrs. Delaney had done many little things, including making Easter baskets for the kids and buying toothpaste and soap for the women. The last activity

Jessie and Mrs. Delaney planned was an event at the park on Fourth of July week. They held a picnic with various activity stations set up for the kids. Many of the women in Mrs. Delaney's garden club volunteered, too. The mothers and their children enjoyed a morning and early afternoon of food and fun.

"Gram," I said impishly, "you and Mom are always baking and cooking way too much stuff for us at the holidays. Even Brandon complains because he finds it hard to keep in shape. What if we did something with Mrs. Delaney for the women's shelter?"

Within a few hours of my comment, Gram and Mom wrote down plans and suggestions for what they could do. When they felt prepared, Mom called Mrs. Delaney to volunteer. She spent almost a half hour on the phone.

"Sharon was so happy and excited with our offer," Mom said. "She worried that she might not be able to handle it by herself. She even thought about cancelling the Christmas lunch. I have to admit, I'm excited about helping."

The three women agreed to meet soon to finalize their plans. My grandmother was really impressed with Sharon Delaney.

"Do you know, Leo," she said with obvious admiration in her voice, "Sharon has already bought gifts for the children and the moms, and she even planted amaryllis bulbs for all of them so that they can watch them bloom? She is an amazing person."

I had to admit that my impression of the Delaney family continued to change dramatically. It wasn't hard to understand how they raised such a wonderful daughter. With Sharon and Dean's support, Jessie had always reached out to others.

I decided I needed to find something to make Jessie proud of me, too. I made a personal promise to continue Jessie's work, first by helping everyone with this Christmas party, but secondly by initiating some new projects of my own.

Chapter 41

MR. DELANEY'S STORY about his true relationship with Jessie haunted me. I replayed it in my head several times a day. My mind went to moments that foreshadowed Jessie's struggle with her adoption and her desire to share her story with me. Memories flashed in my head of times she tried but stopped—times when she hadn't trusted me to be receptive to her feelings.

I related to her struggle because I, too, struggled to share a story. The story of the day she died. Like me, I'm sure there were periods of time where she felt no need to share her story. Would anything change? Aren't some things meant to stay private?

So many secrets—my own and others'—were part of my life. Mrs. Franco was the only person who knew some of my private struggles. When my appointment with her arrived, my apprehension was strong.

As I sat across from Mrs. Franco in her office, I felt much less worried. Perhaps it was the small gold angel pin on the left side of her red turtleneck sweater that comforted me. She had a manila folder on her lap, and her brightly painted red nails curled around it.

"Lee," she said as she smiled, "I'm so glad to see you. Why don't you tell me how you've been doing. I want to hear all about how you've adjusted to school after your suspension."

I forgot that I had not spoken to Mrs. Franco about my return to school. That seemed like weeks ago. So much happened since then that I didn't know where to begin. With her prompting, I began my review of the encounter with Father Mike and Phil Knox. She was relieved that things went so smoothly, and she was genuinely happy at my positive attitude about my school friends.

Eventually I detailed my Saturday afternoon encounter with Mr. Delaney. Her eyes widened in surprise over his revelations. She nodded her head in concern and sympathy for all that had taken place between him and Jessie. I related my last-minute decision not to give Mr. Delaney a copy of the same story I wrote for Mrs. Franco.

As soon as I mentioned the story, her well-manicured nails slid along the side of the folder on her lap. She opened it to reveal the copy I printed for her.

"Yes, Lee," she said as she looked down at the paper. "I'm sure you've been anxious about my response to what you wrote.

That was a complete understatement. Her voice sounded flat, as if she had never read it. Maybe she forgot till now and was just going to do a quick read while I watched. I felt hurt, disappointed, and angry.

She continued to look down at the copy. "So many things that you said in our sessions became much clearer to me once I read this."

Well, at least she read it, I thought. I don't know exactly what I wanted her to do, but I did expect some sort of emotional response, good or bad.

"Before I share my thoughts with you about what you wrote, I need you to do something for me." She hesitated a few seconds. "I want you to carefully read this to yourself."

This time she looked at me as she spoke, and I'm sure she caught the roll of my eyes and my other body language that indicated how I felt. She placed the folder on my lap.

"Now? You want me to read it now? . . . I wrote it. I know what it says."

"Please, do this, Lee. Read it, and read it carefully. Detach yourself, as much as you can, from the emotions of that day. If you can, pretend that you are someone else reading this account. Try to imagine that you are someone who doesn't have a personal attachment to Jessie's death, and you are reading this account for the first time."

Her directions to read my narrative made me realize that I had not thought about Jessie's actual death for several days. In that time I was focused on the suspension, my conversation with Mr. Delaney, and the plans for the women's shelter party. I thought of Jessie all the time, but no images of her death invaded those thoughts.

Mrs. Franco urged me again. "Lee, read this silently to yourself. Pretend it is someone else's story." Her voice sounded hypnotic.

My eyes closed for a brief second, and I sighed audibly. I tried to imagine myself as someone else. Strangely, of all the people who came to my mind—my dad, Jordan, even Father Mike—I decided to channel Mr. Simmons, my homeroom teacher. I recalled his subtle way of making me feel like everything was going to be alright. His easygoing, nonjudgmental attitude made him a teacher who was respected and admired.

I pictured him at his desk as he picked up a manila folder. The folder held an assignment he needed to read and grade. My eyes focused on the words of the narrative.

Jessie and I talked on our cells for about fifteen minutes on the evening before she died. It was close to ten thirty, the time her parents went to bed. Jessie needed to get off the phone and respect the quiet of the house. We still had things to say, so she promised to send me an email before she fell asleep. In the email she asked me to meet her for a walk to the park in the morning.

Rain was in the forecast, but that didn't matter. Jessie wanted to jump in puddles and let the rain hit her face. She teased me with the promise of kisses under the trees in an empty park.

How could I say no? I agreed to meet her around nine o'clock on our special corner that was halfway between our houses.

Rain fell hard all that morning. I remember hearing thunder and seeing flashes of lightning in the early morning hours before I even got out of bed.

The rain continued and didn't slow. So a few minutes before nine, I called Jessie on her cell to make sure she didn't want to cancel. Mr. Delaney was at work, but Mrs. Delaney had the day off. Jessie wanted to get out of the house no matter how badly it was raining. If she hung around, her mom would want her to do a shopping trip for school clothes, and Jessie wasn't in the mood.

I grabbed my hat and put on an old pair of Nikes that were already muddy. I jogged over to our meeting place.

When I approached the corner, I saw Jessie in her yellow rain slicker. She had the hood up to protect her hair. The slicker touched the middle of her upper thigh, and I could just see the hem of khaki shorts underneath. Her bright pink toenails matched her flip-flops.

The rain slowed, but big splashes of raindrops hit the puddles along the sidewalk.

Jessie smiled at me, and her beautiful green eyes sparkled. She reached over and took my hand in hers and gave me a little kiss on the cheek.

"Aren't you glad it's raining, Leo?" As usual, there was a child-like excitement in her voice.

"I think I'd rather see the sun, . . . but if you say so, Jessie, I guess the rain is a good thing."

Just as I said that, the sun came out from behind a cloud. It still rained softly, though; I could hear drops hitting Jessie's slicker.

"Let's take the long way to the park, okay? That way we'll be on the sidewalk. I don't want to get too muddy."

"You're the boss, Jessie. You know I'll go wherever you lead me."

She laughed and tugged my arm in the direction she wanted to go. We walked slowly, and Jessie admired the homes and some of the gardens we saw along the way. She told me the names of some of her favorite flowers and pointed them out as we continued down Elmwood Road. But most of the time we just walked in silence. The only noise was the splash of her feet into some little puddles.

We approached a yard that had a line of hedges all along the sidewalk. They were thick, high, and overgrown. Jessie looked at me with a mischievous grin. She pulled my arm and then gave me a shove that landed me right in the middle of the hedge.

When I pulled myself out of the bush, she pointed at me and laughed. I had hedge pieces all over my shorts, and my baseball hat was still stuck in the bushes.

"How's it feel to be overcome by a girl, Leo?"

She held up her arm like she was flexing her bicep. In a playful, mocking voice she said, "Me the mighty Jessie. You the loser, Leo."

I pulled my hat out of the hedges and put it back on my head. I brushed some lingering pieces of hedge from my shorts. I gave her a fake angry look and said, "Be fearful of Leo the Mighty Lion, beautiful young girl." I growled and put up my hands like clawing lion paws. I snarled at her in my deepest voice.

"You better run; you better hide!"

So strange to me even now. Those were the last words I ever said to her . . . "You better run; you better hide."

She laughed and started running. Her flip-flops slapped against the wet pavement, and splatters of mud hit the back of her tan calves. The slicker hood fell from her head, and her brown hair was swinging back and forth as she ran.

I gave her a head start. I knew she was heading for the tree along the road.

She got close to the tree, and I could see her make a quick turn to get behind it. She was going to use the tree as her shield against the Mighty Lion.

But she never made it that far. Her flip-flops caught on something, maybe the edge of the sidewalk. She fell forward, partially onto the street. She reached for the side of the tree for support, but she missed. Her reach set her even more off balance.

Then . . . the car, the car came out of nowhere. I don't even remember hearing it approach.

At the funeral parlor people talked about the accident. I heard over and over the whispers about how the impact of the car killed Jessie instantly. "What a blessing," some said. "At least she didn't suffer." Other people discussed how sorry they felt for the man who hit her. "He'll carry that guilt with him for the rest of his life."

But I'm the guilty one. Jessie would not have fallen into the path of that car if I hadn't uttered those awful words. "You better run; you better hide." And, I'm the one who has to carry that burden for the rest of my life.

I finished the story and pictured Mr. Simmons placing the papers back in the folder, just as I was doing right now. Mrs. Franco spoke warily when she realized I was done.

"Are you alright, Lee?"

I nodded as I clutched the folder in my hands. What did Mrs. Franco expect to happen when I reviewed the account of my last days with Jessie? Was she just trying to assess my reactions as she watched me read?

When she finally spoke, she sounded like an attorney making concluding statements to a jury.

"Lee, you can't continue to blame yourself for Jessie's death. If you're going to take the leap of blaming yourself, you might as well blame Jessie for her own death. She was the one who wanted to go for the walk . . . she chose the street to go on . . . she provoked you into pretending to chase her. The driver ran off the road, Lee. Jessie could have fallen by that tree and not been killed if that driver had not gone off the road. No one, Lee—not me, not your parents, not the Delaneys—would ever blame you for the mistake of someone who lost control of his car."

I began to cry. The tears were hot and burning as they rolled down my cheeks. I felt so much pain. I missed Jessie so much. Just one more kiss, just one more hug, one more "I love you." I couldn't stop the tears, and I covered my eyes with my hands and bent my head almost to my lap.

For all these months, I had focused so much on my guilt that I avoided the bigger picture of what was really hurting me. I would never hold Jessie again. I would never see the sparkle of her green eyes. I would never again have anyone love me in the way that Jessie loved me.

Mrs. Franco slipped some tissue into my hands. She stood beside me for a moment and touched me lightly on the shoulder. She sat back in her chair and waited for me to speak.

"I miss her so much," I finally managed to say. The tears dripped from my eyes. "I loved her, and she was my best friend . . . I loved her so much."

My emotions overcame me. I zoned out into some universe that was a cross between a nightmare world and a fever state. My eyes stayed closed, but I was acutely aware of the bright lights in Mrs. Franco's office. My tears stopped flowing from my eyes, but I had the odd sensation that they were flooding into my brain. My head hurt; my heart hurt. I couldn't think, and I didn't want to think.

I heard the soft whisper of Mrs. Franco's voice. "Lee, Lee . . . drink some water."

Her hand spread open my fingers and pushed a glass into my grip. I sipped the water carefully as I slowly opened my eyes and tried to focus on my surroundings. My heart pulsed in my throat, and my breathing was erratic and painful.

I sipped some more water and gradually began to calm. Mrs. Franco took the empty glass from my hand, and then we sat in silence for several minutes before she spoke again.

"Lee, your sadness is making its way into the open. All these months, you have used a coping mechanism called "deflection" for your grief. It is something you are quite good at. Deflection helps in many ways. What you did was avoid your grief over Jessie's death by punishing yourself with guilt. You diverted the real pain of your loss by convincing yourself that it was your fault that Jessie was hit by that car. You do realize, don't you, that it is not your fault that Jessie died?"

I shrugged my shoulders in an attempt to indicate that I agreed somewhat to the statement. All my guilt hadn't magically disappeared. I wished so badly that I had never teased her into running. But I accepted that my teasing threat to Jessie was only one of many elements that resulted in her death.

I looked down at the folder on my lap. It was speckled with tears and had a small water ring from my glass. I handed the folder and papers back to Mrs. Franco.

Chapter 42

MY DAD WAS WAITING in the car. If he noticed my red eyes, he didn't say anything.

"Penguins pulled out another win, Leo," he said as he adjusted the radio dial. "What do you say about taking in a game over Christmas vacation? I'll talk to one of the guys at work. He has season tickets and usually goes out of town for the holidays."

"I think I'd really like that, Dad," I managed to say with genuine enthusiasm. "Nothin' says Christmas like a good hockey game."

That evening I went to my room and sat at my desk. I opened the drawer that held the stored treasures of my brief time with Jessie. The wrinkled copy of my narrative, the one I had thought about sharing with Mr. Delaney, rested on top of the brown leather journal. Carefully I placed both items on my desktop and opened the cover of the journal.

To Leo from Jessie.
Fill this book with all the good thoughts
that I know are inside your heart.

My hands smoothed the wrinkled paper and folded it neatly in half. I slid the story between the back cover and the last page. I gently straightened the many other papers of poetry that I kept in the journal.

My fingertips caressed the cover, and I thought of the touch of Jessie's hand in mine. Would the pain of her loss ever go away?

I reached into my treasure drawer again and pulled out the sparkled tissue paper. Just as Jessie had done for me two years ago, I wrapped the journal. It fit smoothly into the red and white striped Christmas bag.

Maybe in a few months or years, I would fill those blank pages with our poetry. I might even add the story of my last days with Jessie and perhaps wonder why I had felt so responsible for her death. But, there was no hurry to fill the journal. No future wedding or birthday celebration when Jessie would be touched by my thoughtful and loving gesture. The warmth of her grateful kiss would never touch my cheek.

My digital clock flashed ten. I felt Jessie's presence as I tucked the bag gently into the back of the drawer and whispered into the air, "I love you, Jessie. I miss you with all my heart."

EPILOGUE

CHRISTMAS WITHOUT JESSIE was difficult, but it was not without joy and memorable moments. Many new holiday traditions started that year.

Mom and Dad invited the Delaneys to join us on Christmas Eve. Sharon and Dean arrived at our home around five, and the Schillings came shortly after. We extended the group even more by inviting my friend Jordan and his father, Sam.

Everyone brought some type of food. Grandma Lily and Mom made a ham and a turkey with stuffing. The Delaneys brought scalloped potatoes and rolls. The Schillings arrived with assorted vegetable sides and appetizers. Jordan and his dad supplied wine, soda, and snacks. The buffet of food overflowed our kitchen island and counters. Assorted cookies, pies, candy, and snacks lined the bar in our family room.

My dad shoved some Christmas CDs into our sound system, and soon the house smelled and sounded like Christmas.

The evening began with a formal air, but by seven o'clock the noise level of conversations was impressive.

Sam Kessler had Jordan's weird sense of humor and kept everyone laughing at his ridiculous childhood stories. Jordan spent most of the evening trying to hit on

Nicole and Michelle Schilling. Luckily they had a good sense of humor about his amorous attempts. Brandon even took Jordan aside for some brotherly advice about the dos and don'ts of trying to pick up girls.

Grandma, Mom, Karen Schilling, and Sharon were like a little sorority. They giggled and talked at the kitchen table and obviously had a great time.

Eventually Dean and my dad discovered some common topics that excited them both. They were both opinionated about government and politics and enjoyed a few friendly debates about current events. Mr. Delaney revealed his passion for hockey. Once he and Dad started a conversation on the Pittsburgh Penguins and the NHL, Brandon and I joined the conversation too.

Around ten, Dad gathered everyone in the family room. Our Christmas tree glistened with lights, the fireplace glowed warmly, and holiday carols played softly in the background. Dad made sure that everyone had a glass of champagne, and then he stood by the Christmas tree to make a toast.

"Christmas is a season of family and friends, and I have never felt as blessed with both as I do right now. This has been a difficult year. We lost someone, and that loss left a big hole in our hearts. Our dear Jessie will always be missed. But our connection to her is what brought us all together tonight. So, I ask you all to raise your glasses and drink to our new friendships and to the life of Jessie Delaney. May her life inspire us to show the type of kindness and love that she showed to everyone she met."

Mr. Delaney walked to my dad. He lifted his glass to my dad's and whispered, "Thank you, Wayne. Thank you so much. You can't imagine how much your family has helped us heal."

Mark Schilling approached the two of them and clinked his glass with Dad's and then Dean's. He smiled and began singing in his melodious voice.

"O, Christmas tree, O Christmas tree, how beautiful your branches . . ."

Dad chimed in quickly, and, to everyone's surprise, Sharon Delaney harmonized beautifully with them. Tissues were pulled from pockets, eyes were wiped of tears, and hands reached out to touch someone nearby. Mom grabbed me and Brandon, and she hugged our waists as we listened to the harmony of the trio.

I felt Jessie's presence as surely as I felt my mother's hug. She would always be with me; she would always be my love.

My mom kissed my cheek and squeezed me closer to her. My dad smiled at us from across the room.

I counted my many blessings. I had a wonderful family and good friends. I shared a small part of my life with Jessie and experienced her friendship and love. My heart whispered a prayer of thanks. And, for the first time in a very long while, I felt that God was listening.

THE END

For more information or to contact
Lorraine Roposh Beran

email: lorrainelberan@gmail.com
twitter: @beranlorraine
blog: rainydaypublications.wordpress.com

WA